THE ROGUE'S GALAXY

The Infinity Project Book One

ERIN HAYES

Erin Hayes Books

The Rogue's Galaxy - © 2017, 2019 Erin Hayes

All Right Reserved

No part of this book may be used or reproduced without the written permission of the author.

This is a work of fiction. Names, characters, places, and incidents are either the product of the author's imagination or are used fictitiously. Any resemblance to actual persons (living or dead) is entirely coincidental.

Cover art by Design by Definition
Edited by Lindsay Galloway of Contagious Edits

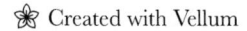

❀ Created with Vellum

Chapter 1

Every time I plug myself into a computer, I feel a jolt of electricity shoot up from the finger connected to the port, through my arm. It ends with an unpleasant sizzle at the back of my tongue, singeing all my taste buds. I won't be able to taste my coffee for a week after this. Coffee is the only thing that makes me bearable at 0900 hours.

I hate this part of the job.

I must be making a face, because the second mate PC snorts loudly, putting a hand on his hip. "Not enjoyin' that, Clem?" he drawls, aiming his zapper with his other hand at our tied-up hostages. The three men glare at him over their cloth gags—we're super high-tech here.

"You're not the one who's assimilating with the ship," I mutter, even as PC continues to snicker.

"I hope the ship makes you breakfast in the morning," he replies, and our shipmates Taka, Daisy, and Captain Louis chuckle in answer.

Cocky bastards. All they have to do is hold out until I've gathered everything. Taka's soldering the door shut, Daisy is monitoring the radar for incoming ships, and Captain Louis is keeping tabs on our own ship docked here.

"Clem, hurry," the old man grumbles to me. He never likes leaving Orion, our android navigator, in charge of his ship.

I roll my eyes in annoyance, using my mechanical right eye to read through the streams of data that are now running through the wires of my cyborg half. I sift through the data—seriously, it's amazing how much shit people will put on computers without proper firewalls. Sure, I can easily break through most firewalls in less than three nanoseconds, but I'm always surprised at just what people have that isn't protected.

Here, I read all the bios of the crew members on this vessel —*the STS Nautilus*, how obvious!—and I can read their paystubs going back to their births. Some of the crews are employees for life here.

"Syn-Tech gives you guys *great* pay raises," I say, looking at the tied-up members of the crew with my right eye. "Although, Parker," I add, pointing at the first mate as I read his file, scrolling past the retinas of my right eye, "If I were you, I'd ask for an 11.47% pay raise to put yourself on the same scale as the second mate. Then again, you can't really compete with the captain's younger cousin."

I see Parker blink in shock at my words and then glare at the man next to him. The captain, presumably, although I'm sure it's Syn-Tech who decides what they're paid. That's how it goes for Lifers, as we Free Agents call them—if you're born on a planet or a space station under the control of a corporation, your entire existence is owned by that corporation, including pay raises, promotional opportunities, even which lavatories you're allowed to shit in.

Fuck that.

Life in outer space without the safety and protection of corporations may be rough, but we're at least in charge of our own destiny. To an extent.

At the moment, I'm working for Farer-Prime, a rival corporation to Syn-Tech. At least until I find the information they hired my crew to downloot and relay back to them in exchange for 45 million Space Yen. And then a corporation like Yarvis-5 will hire us to downloot another company's ship for corporate espionage, like some old Earthian game of tennis.

Not that I've ever played tennis. You have to have a court and reliable gravity for that.

I continue searching until I change to the directory:
/Cordinates

"Ahhh," I breathe in satisfaction. "Your technology officer misspelled 'coordinates' in the folder name." I give a mock-disapproving click of my tongue. "That actually tripped me up for a few minutes there, which is pretty good. Although I'd be worried about locating any other files with that track record."

My mechanical side wades through the files, grabbing all the latest coordinates of every freighter, private ship, space station, and warehouse in this sector of space. The information will only be relevant for seventy-two hours at most. That's why it's imperative that we get this relayed to them as soon as possible. Once Syn-Tech finds out that their information is compromised, they'll scramble all their coordinates, making it impossible for Farer-Prime to locate and destroy their property. And they'll retaliate with a similar gambit.

Such a petty game, this whole thing.

At least it pays well. My cyborg foot has been acting up lately, and I woke up in my barracks last night with my right leg just randomly kicking the wall. It made a dent, so I have no idea how long it was doing that. But it does mean that something is fried in there.

New cyborg feet cost at least 50 million Space Yen, so I have a few more runs to downloot before I can afford it.

Not for the first time, I wish I were an android so I wouldn't have to eat. Not that they get paid anyways.

"Clem?" Captain Louis asks, glancing back at me. He's starting to sweat.

Yeah, yeah. We tripped the alarm on our way in, so we have about T-minus 158.7 seconds before we'll be descended upon by Syn-Tech fighters.

"I'm downloading now," I grit to Louis as I tell the computer to copy the directory onto my local drive—*me*. "Files take as long as they have to duplicate. Hold your horses."

"I've never ridden a horse," Taka muses as he tears some more wires from the wall. Another airlock seals shut, making another barrier between us and the *Nautilus's* crew trying to make it to the bridge. He's a slight, wiry man with prosthetics for both arms and bleached hair. "They had them on old Earth, right? Big mammals, majestic creatures?"

"Apparently, they pissed a lot," Daisy says, not taking her eyes off the screens. "Hence the saying, 'Piss like a racehorse.'"

Leave it to her to ruin Taka's beautiful vision of our home planet, which we've never seen. Daisy's a big woman in her late forties with tattoos all over her body, her red hair streaked with gray and pulled up into a severe bun. She's not zaftig so much as just built like a tank. Her legs are cyborg, but her voluptuous breasts are all real, and I know a great many people who lose at arm wrestling with her all the time.

"If we get out of here alive, I'll buy you a simulation," Captain Louis tersely says to Taka. Because if we *don't* get out of here, Syn-Tech fighters will blow up our ship, and we'll be burned to a crisp.

They usually get very angry in the heat of the moment—obviously, because we're stealing from them. And then, in a few weeks, it'll blow over and they'll hire us for a similar job.

The life of a space pirate.

We have four rules: Never kill anyone, only take what you were hired to get, delete what you get after delivery so you never have to worry about blackmail, and maintain loyalty to the crew above all else. That's why Captain Louis runs such a tight ship—it's me as the first mate, PC as the boatswain, our navigator Orion, mechanic Daisy, engineer Taka, Venice Moon our cook, and a little cabin boy named Oliver Twist that Captain Louis took in three months ago. I have to admit, the old man has a big heart. It's how PC and I ended up with him.

Granted, it's also how I became a pirate myself.

My retina displays confirmation that I've successfully copied over all the files in the folder, and my internal diagnostics make sure that there are no viruses or malware now in my system. One time, I downloaded a trojan virus that caused my artificial lungs to stop working for a week, and I battled a case of pneumonia that antibiotics couldn't fix.

I don't have time to wait, though.

"We're good," I say, giving a curt nod to Captain Louis. I call back my middle finger, the one that's connected to the hard drive of the *Nautilus*. My robotic hand swallows up the cables, and I make a fist.

Everything seems to be in order.

"All right," Captain Louis barks, "we have T-minus 120 seconds—"

"118.78," I correct before cringing at the reflex. I hate it when the computer part of my brain takes over my cognitive functions.

Louis glares at me for a moment we don't have to waste before he sighs and motions for all of us to run for the far hatch. Taka touches two wires to each other, and the door irises open, just as the schematics said they would. Then all we have is a quick run to the airlock and then we're back on the *Pícara* and back in FTL before Syn-Tech gets here.

That's the idea anyways.

I get to my feet, grabbing my zapper, and I follow PC's big form as we jog through the hatch, leaving the crew tied up on the bridge. They'll be found and released by the Syn-Tech fighters soon, so I'm not too worried about them.

As for the rest of the crew, I just hope they don't find us on the run to our ship. Our zappers may be set to stun, but I'm pretty sure theirs aren't. People get really pissed when you steal their stuff, even if it is a bunch of 1s and 0s. They'll even go so far as to shoot to kill. I lost a kidney because of that. The corporation funding us that time paid me an extra million Space Yen as recompense. Too bad a real kidney costs twice that much, so it's another piece of me that's machine instead of human. Pretty soon, I'll be more robot than Orion.

We run to the airlock with Daisy leading us. For how big she is, she certainly runs through the *Nautilus* like a sprinter, her booming voice announcing her trek through the hallways as she shoots anyone that gets in her way. PC and I exchange glances, reminding ourselves not to piss her off. Ever. She got mad when I took her fork in the mess hall, and Captain Louis had to intervene before she pummeled me into space dust.

"T-Minus 47 seconds until we are intercepted by Syn-Tech fighters." I grit my teeth as I hear Orion's silky, calm voice in my ear. Whoever programmed him initially must have thought that having a navigator with a sexy voice would be a nice change. He doesn't sound hurried or concerned. If anything, he sounds almost bored.

Captain Louis doesn't, though. "Hurry, hurry, hurry!" he barks back at us.

We're running out of time, and I know that everyone will blame me if we get fired at. I couldn't help it if the damn technology officer had misspelled the folder name and that the folder was several terabytes large. Not a huge file by today's standards, but my bandwidth is only so much. I feel those terabytes in my stomach, like I've just had a huge dinner. I can't wait to purge and upload this shit, as it's making me feel bloated and lazy.

I touch my earpiece. "Be ready to take us into FTL, Orion."

"Already have the coordinates set as per Captain Louis's orders," he tells me.

Smug bastard, I think to myself. As First Mate, I can't command him to do anything, especially if it goes against Louis's direct orders. Orion takes every chance to remind me that I can't just order him to do something.

We turn the corner, and I nearly hurrah at the sight of the airlock. Taka is already inputting the information for the airlock to open. It does iris open, and Daisy is the first to reenter our ship.

I hear voices in the hall behind us, coming up ever so quickly. I don't tell PC or Captain Louis, but I shift my trajectory just a little bit so that I'm blocking everyone from our assailants, just in case we're fired upon.

Hopefully it won't come to that.

We have just a little further and…

A blast fires behind me, and my sensors on the cyborg half of my body go off. I don't feel pain necessarily, but I can feel the sparks in my right leg as a blast from an enemy zapper shreds through my right thigh. Alarms and warnings go off on my retinas, and my leg stops working.

I stumble into PC, who catches me by one arm. He mutters a curse under his breath as he shoots behind us, catching my assailant in the chest and stunning him.

Yep, even though my leg is as good as a bench right now, we still don't shoot to kill.

"You stupid, stupid, stupid—" he mutters.

"You're welcome," I tell him through gritted teeth as he drags me along. "Just think, if this hit you, you'd be bleeding out right now."

I see a muscle in his jaw twitch as we finally cross the

threshold onto the *Pícara*, and Taka pounds on the airlock, sealing us away from Syn-Tech's forces.

"Get us out of here, Orion!" Captain Louis thunders into his communicator.

"Sir—" Even to me, the android sounds a little concerned. We're not buckled in for FTL speeds…

"I don't care," Louis shouts as he wraps his hand around a stray strap and turns on his Grav-Boots as his only restraints. "If we wait any longer, they're going to fire on us, and we won't have a ship!" Daisy and Taka do the same, grabbing onto anything they can to secure them in the initial speed boost.

"Roger that," Orion intones, all concern gone from his voice.

I watch as PC grabs onto a handle, his teeth gritted. I try reaching for it and turning on the Grav functions in my cyborgs, but I'm too late, and my right leg still isn't working.

The *Pícara* hits FTL, and I'm flung from PC's grip. Of course, when I bump my head against the unforgiving metal ceiling, it's the biological part, and stars dance across my vision before I'm thrust into a darkness deeper than any black hole.

Just another success for the crew of the *Pícara*.

Chapter 2

PC is still calling me stupid when I wake up. He's very creative with it, too.

"Clementine, you stupid, stupid, stupid…"

I grimace and manage to stick my tongue out at him. "Nice to hear that you care, Popcorn," I say amusedly, using his real name.

It's only fair since he just used my full name. I see his cheeks flush deep red at the mention of his parents' horrible name for him. Our names are Clementine and Popcorn, following a trend to name kids after exotic foods from old Earth.

PC told me when he found out that it was a buttery, greasy snack, he was mortified and immediately shortened it. Clementine is only marginally better, but at least it's a fruit.

I think it is, at least. I've never seen one in person.

I put my cyborg hand to my forehead and groan. "What happened?"

"When we hit FTL, you conked your head," Captain Louis says grimly. I hadn't even known he was in this room. "You blacked out."

"Yeah, yeah. Story of my life." I try pushing myself to sit up, but PC puts a big hand on my chest and forces me back down. I can see why.

Taka is working on the giant gaping hole in my leg, so entranced by all my inner workings of my robotic pieces. I see the data flashing in his own cyborg eyes as he tries to analyze what's broken in my leg. "Thanks, Taka," I murmur.

He merely gives a disinterested wave. Taka lives in a fantasy world where we can't reach him most days. He's either fully immersed in robotics and computers or dreaming about life on old Earth. He's rarely ever in the here and now.

And with how crappy the here and now can be, I don't blame him. Whereas I struggle with how much of me is human versus robot, I think he wishes he'd been assembled instead of born. Life may have been kinder on him in that case.

"How does it look, doc?" I ask.

"Your circuits are fried," Taka says. "I can patch you up to a decent state, but you're going to need to get that new foot as soon as possible."

Of course. I need another few runs at least before I have enough saved up to get a new foot. And that would wipe out all of my savings for the foreseeable future. So much for retiring early.

"Ow," I mutter, flinching on reflex. My right foot twitches in response, my toes curling with the pain. "I think sensory functions are back online at least."

Taka gives a demure smile.

"How long have I been out?" I ask Captain Louis. We only have a three-hour window of when we're supposed to pull out of FTL to transfer our data. If I've been out for longer than that, then we could be missing out on our huge payment. Someone like Taka or Orion could dig through my memory banks for the data, but doing that is a severe invasion of privacy.

And there are certainly things in there that I don't want *anyone* seeing.

"You've been out for an hour," Louis answers, and I sigh in relief. "Are the files damaged?"

I hide my smile as I quickly run diagnostics on my memory banks. Now that I'm back to my snarky self, Louis puts up his pretense of detachedness. He cares about his team, but if we're out of danger, he starts to pretend to play captain again.

"All files are accounted for," I say, relieved.

At least my hard drives are harder than my head.

Louis nods. "Think you can upload it to Farer-Prime, then?"

I twirl my right ankle once, and Taka lets out a surprised noise. I must be recovering quicker than he thought possible.

"Of course. Might just need some help."

AMUSINGLY, it's not my leg that's giving me trouble walking; it's my head. I can't seem to keep things from spinning and matching up with itself, and it's making my inner gyroscope mess up and it thinks I'm in a tailspin.

Which I am, I suppose. "Fucking head," I mutter.

"It's what you get for having a bio-head," PC says amusedly. He should know the benefits—he has a metal plate on one side, which covers most of his skull.

"Shut up," I say, and he snickers softly.

He helps me hobble my way to the bridge, where I can set up a secure line to Farer-Prime and upload the files. The bridge isn't too fancy, just a dual-level room with one wall open to the sea of stars beyond us.

As we enter at the lower level, classical music hits my ears. It's played over the loud speakers in the bridge, filling every space with violins. I pause, waiting for the computer side of my brain to identify the song as I've never heard it before.

"It is Antonio Vivaldi's *Le quattro stagioni*," a familiar voice says, before I can come up with an answer. "Otherwise known as *The Four Seasons*. Particularly *L'inverno*, movement 1."

Ahead of us, a taut, rigid figure with his back to us turns around and gives us a smile that's not exactly cold, but it doesn't necessarily reach his eyes. Orion is an interesting android in that he's somewhere in between a full robot and a human. Sometimes, he can come across as more human than Taka, and at others, he's more robotic than a zapper.

Looks like we caught him in the middle of one of his latter moments.

"It's pretty," I admit as the violins raise in a crescendo. "I've never heard it before."

A muscle twitches in Orion's cheek, and I wonder if he's trying to smile or if there's a malfunction in his cheek. There's something uncanny about androids that you can just never put your finger on.

Sure, Orion looks human enough, but he's almost too perfect. He stands at six-and-a-half feet tall, with a body built with simulated muscle. His skin is a deep umber that catches the light from the stars flashing by us in the window. A chiseled jaw and sculpted cheekbones round out his features under his shock of thick, coarse black hair.

An Orion-class android was meant to be more of an escort than a navigator, and looking at him, you can believe that every woman and man's fantasy could come true with him.

"You're trying to outclass us, Orion," PC says as he helps me over to my chair.

The android frowns. "How so?"

PC winks at me. "You just have better taste in music."

The muscle twitches again in Orion's cheek. "All music is a

form of math," he explains. "And the reason why this must sound more pleasant is because—"

"Yeah, yeah," Captain Louis says gruffly, causing Orion to look at him. "We get it. Take us out of FTL so Clem can upload the data before our cut-off. We've already had a few hiccups with today's run, so I'd like to send off this data and purge it as soon as possible."

Orion hesitates for the briefest moment before clasping his hands behind his back and snapping his feet together. "Of course, sir."

Captain Louis rolls his eyes. No matter how many times he tells Orion to stop calling him "sir," he keeps doing it. It's a part of Orion's programming.

We all strap ourselves in. Everyone that is, except for Orion, who can hold himself straight up with the Grav-functions in his feet.

"Everyone, please prepare for deceleration," he says into the intercom. Somewhere on the *Pícara*, Venice Moon, Oliver Twist, and Daisy are strapping themselves in.

After a few heartbeats, I feel the sedative prick my human left arm, feeding me drugs that will keep my heart from exploding with the sudden deceleration. Faster than light is an amazing advancement—we can travel across the galaxy in the matter of a few months, but the human body can't handle it as well as we'd like.

A part of me resents that fragility in me. The other part wants to hold onto it as much as possible. Because the more human I can be, the less I feel like a fraud.

"Go for it, Orion," Louis says from the captain's chair.

The android nods and pulls the lever towards him, and I can feel the shift in the *Pícara* all the way from every cell in my body crying out from the change, as well as the nuts and bolts rattling themselves apart within me. My vision blurs with the sudden headache, and I wonder if it's from knocking my head or if it's from the ship braking so damn hard.

Both are possibilities.

Maybe *this* is the part I most hate about my job.

"Clem," Louis says. He sounds as winded as I feel. "Open up a com and start uploading to Farer-Prime. We're running out of time."

"On it." I extend my right hand and call out the port on my middle finger. I insert it into the hub, feeling that similar tingling feeling ricochet through my body. My tongue is fried again, and it feels like I'm breathing smoke.

I take it back. *This* is definitely the part of the job I hate the most.

It doesn't help that the *Picara* isn't a big fan of me assimilating with her. She views me as an invading entity and constantly tries to kick me out of her system. It's not that I can't fight back or anything, but I don't want to make an enemy out of the very spaceship I live on. One time I had to bypass her security protocols to upload a dangerous file, and I had to deal with cold showers every day that week.

I've told Taka and Captain Louis about it many times, but they've called me crazy for it. The ship isn't supposed to have a personality or AI, and I understand that what I experience should be impossible. But it totally isn't. It's unlike any other ship I've assimilated with.

It makes me wonder if there's more to computers and AI than I know. Orion's indicative of that. And I catch him watching me.

I swallow back the bad taste in my mouth and continue typing in my uplink password with my left hand. Finally, I join their server.

"We're uploading to Farer-Prime," I say, as I command myself to grab everything from "/cordinates" and copy it. I'm ready to purge myself of this information as soon as possible so

I can clear out my memory banks and run at full efficiency once again.

Well, except for my busted leg.

"And in time, too," PC says approvingly. He's watching the loading form to see the estimates for when the packet will be delivered. *Just* in the nick of time, it seems. I breathe a sigh of relief and sit back in my chair, letting my cyborg body do the rest of its business. There's no further communication between us and Farer-Prime, because to do so will be an admission that we were doing business together, which the other corporations wouldn't like.

Even though they all do it. It's like they avoid any association because they don't want to admit they're no better than everyone else. We get our jobs through encrypted messages, and we receive payments through unknown sources.

It's how the world works. At least ours as space pirates.

I feel the ding through my body as I'm alerted that the transfer is complete. I glance over at PC, who looks down at his console. A wide grin spreads across his face. "We're now 45 million Space Yen richer."

There's a collective sigh of relief throughout the *Pícara*. Still though, I can't help but grumble.

"Should've asked for more," I say to Louis. "After all, I got shot. *Again*." I can't seem to stay out of zappers' ways, whether it's going for a loot run or just running to get some food. I tend to piss people off.

"Your kidney injury happened on a Farer-Prime run as well," Orion says thinly before Louis can respond. "It was wise of Captain Louis to not bring that up, or else they'd start thinking we're running a scam here."

"We *are* running a scam," I point out to him as I cross my arms. "And that *was* Farer-Prime last time? All these different corporations are blurring together."

Orion nods, his full lips pressed to a thin line. I wonder

what it would be like to kiss those lips, but I avert my attention away from him and look at Louis. "What do you think of that?" I ask him point-blank.

He chuckles dryly. "I agree with Orion," he says. "You got a rather large payout last time."

"It was only enough to cover my pain pills after my kidney replacement," I retort.

"Just a hazard of the job," PC says with a shrug. "Other Free Agents aren't so lucky."

I don't have a reply for that. It's widely known that life without a corporation to protect you is much harsher. I go to some space ports and see Free Agents missing limbs or using very old equipment to keep their bodies running. If you're not a space pirate, you're either a space junk collector, water distiller, selling your body, or farming on an asteroid with shitty, infertile soil. Most decide to *not* go the space pirate route, mainly because they don't like getting shot at.

Then again, I've earned more money in this one run than any of them will ever see in their lives.

Daisy is the only one of us who was born a Lifer, underneath the banner of Kavelin Works. She left when she was fifteen years old and refuses to talk about her time there.

Then again, I don't have a memory of life before Captain Louis found me. Maybe I was a Lifer, too, at one point. I look down at my cyborg hand and make a fist. All through my body, I have metal and wires, a lot of it necessary to keep me alive. 52.8% of me is machine, making me have more in common with Orion than anyone else. The replacement kidney brought me over that line. The others on the *Pícara* may have cyborg parts, but I have the most. It's not a game I want to win.

I hate it. I feel like I'm losing my humanity. At what point do I become a cyborg with human parts instead of the other way around?

If I lived as a Lifer, would I be in better shape?

I'm still contemplating how different life would have been if I'd been born underneath the banner of a corporation when Venice Moon rings the dinner bell. Seriously, it's a triangle that he dings over the intercom. Sometimes you can't take tradition away from a man.

"Food's ready," the old man gruffs before shutting off the link.

And that's how all meals start on the *Pícara*.

Chapter 3

"I'm going to get me one of those robotic dogs," Daisy announces around her mouthful of food. Today, it's some kind of colorless mush. Venice Moon is a good cook, but we don't give him much to work with in terms of ingredients. Usually, he's working off MREs and recycled food.

"A dog?" Oliver Twist asks, his eyes big and round. The boy is only around nine years old with copper skin and huge, expressive eyes. He's the only member of the crew with his body intact. I'll do everything I can to keep it that way. I know Daisy will too. She's grown close to him since Louis took him in a year ago after finding him in a dumpster on a space port.

Daisy gives him a good-natured nod. It's strange seeing the big, scowly woman so tender with the little boy. That maternal instinct is present, even in her. Oliver's innocence has really smoothed out her rough patches.

"After this run, I have enough saved up," she says to him with a wink. "Maybe one of those big brown models. Or a wee little barky one. What do you think?"

Oliver gives an excited yip, covering up his mouth with his hands.

"I won't have a little shit running around the ship barking at us and marking his territory with oil," Captain Louis mutters as he spoons out another helping of mashed *something*. He sprinkles some salt over it. Salt's really hard to come by, and we only use it in extreme situations. I can tell from Venice's frown that it doesn't escape him.

So I keep the conversation going before the cook threatens to quit again. "If Oliver keeps an eye on the dog and trains him," I say, grabbing a forkful of my own meal, "then that shouldn't be a problem. Will it, buddy?"

He shakes his head. "I'll look after him. Please?"

I see Louis's resolve waver and hide my grin by shoveling the fork into my mouth. Oh, that is *foul*. My eyes water as I remind myself that over half of my body isn't being poisoned by this meal. If only my tongue were mechanical—I could try to change the taste profiles within my computing systems, but I think that may screw up a few other things.

I learned a long time ago not to mess with my internal status quo.

"Fine," Louis mutters before he adds pepper to his meal. I'm thinking about doing the same. Desperate times call for desperate measures.

Taka eats his meal without any fuss or making a face. I think he's probably trying to solve some sort of mathematical problem in his head. He does that when he's quiet.

To my right, PC eats in silence but only because he's looking at the news on his mini-tab, a companion device that can be used to access the Net or play different forms of media. He always likes to catch up on the events that are happening in the wider galaxy.

I try to avoid it as much as possible. Keep everything as close as possible to Clementine Jones's world, and I'll be happy.

Across from me, I see Orion watching us with a curious expression on his face. As an android, he doesn't have to eat like the rest of us, which, for once, I'm jealous. He sits bolt upright and only speaks when spoken to. I bet he wants to go back to the bridge and listen to some more Vivaldi.

"What are you thinking?" I ask him, point-blank.

He blinks at me. "Thinking?"

"Yeah," I say, twirling my fork to indicate the whole table. "It's when your processor runs through a few different functions and computations to mull over some problems. Or it could be that you're running through the probabilities of what you'll be doing later. Or contemplating the bigger things in the universe. *Thinking*."

Orion's mouth curves up slightly. "Not much," he says cryptically.

Of course. I nearly growl into my bowl of food. It's been a shitty day.

"Holy space balls!" PC shouts as he scrolls to another article on his mini-tab.

"Language," Louis mutters, even though he has the worst mouth out of us all. He's been trying to teach Oliver some manners, but that's been a challenge for him because of his foul vocabulary.

PC doesn't seem to hear him, though, as he scrolls through the news article. "It's gone!"

I frown, leaning over the mini-tab to see what the hell he's talking about. "What's gone?"

"Syn-Tech Port Delta," he says. He taps on the screen, and the mini-tab opens up a hologram in the middle of the table, illuminating all our faces and the shadows of the mess hall. In front of us is a three-dimensional map of a space station in the 4th Galactic Quadrant in the Milky Way. A few pieces of information pop up, that the space port is home to over half a million people, that they manufacture pharmaceuticals, and that over 95% of the population are Lifers—people born under the Syn-Tech umbrella.

Then the headline flashes over the whole diagram: VIRUS KILLS ENTIRE POPULATION OF SPACE STATION. NO SURVIVORS.

I narrow my eyes. "What?" Daisy curses under her breath, and Taka just blinks at it curiously. Orion's eyes are narrowed as well, and I can see that he's saving the data in his memory banks based on the movement of his mechanical eyes.

Space is a dangerous place. Every new territory that humankind discovers is another chance for us to encounter something deadly, whether it's asteroids, alien-life, warped time scales due to gravity, and more. Many, many people die every day from something like this. Except usually in a space port as big as Delta, there are measures in place to protect the populace.

It's rare that something this big ever happens.

PC is still scrolling through his mini-tab as he continues to read through the article. "Says that some freighters brought it with them, and it wiped out the whole space station in a matter of days."

"Do they know what virus?" Taka asks dazedly.

After a moment, PC shakes his head. "No."

Louis sits forward with his hands clasped. "Is it quarantined, then?"

"Says so right here." PC looks at the diagram again. "The Feds are planning on nuking the whole place and have eliminated any escapees who could possibly carry the virus away from the port."

A feeling of dread settles in at that last revelation. The Feds are a cross-organizational group created for the sole purpose of law enforcement. The different corporations combined to come up with something akin to a police force to cover vast swaths of space, and they're decent fellows for the most part. They're already bribe-able, though, and they acquiesce to the requests of whatever corporation's territory they're in.

A nuclear blast and killing any survivors is a last resort to keep the infection from spreading. No doubt there'd be space pirates like us heading there right now to strip the place clean of all information, a dangerous gamble even we wouldn't take.

"So they're really frightened then," I murmur, feeling my stomach drop at the words.

Oliver makes a frightened little noise, and Daisy wraps a beefy arm around his shoulders. I wonder if there is a better place to talk about this, not around the mess table. I hate to give the poor kid nightmares. Stars know we all have our night-time terrors.

PC shakes his head, oblivious to the kid's distress. "Nothing about that."

"Well," Louis says, wiping his mouth with a napkin, "so long as that space port is at least a quadrant away from us, then there's no need for us to worry about it. We'll be fine. I think I'm done with dinner," he says, getting to his feet. Venice's face falls that the captain cut short his dinner, but he hopefully realizes that we've all lost our appetites and not just because of the food. "Daisy, Oliver," he says softly, before turning away, "you can get your dog. But the second I find an oil slick…"

The little boy shrieks excitedly and gives Louis a hug around the knees. "Thank you, sir! I promise, he won't do anything. Daisy!" he exclaims, looking back at the woman. Daisy only grins and nods.

"I think it's time for you to get to bed," Louis says, picking up the boy with a sigh. The boy hugs himself to the captain as he's carried out, completely content with his life.

At least Oliver's attention is diverted from the tragedy at hand. Still, though, I can't get the thought out of my head. *Half a million people, killed in just a few days.* How does that even happen? I thought that we were more resilient than that, that there were more measures put in place to keep an apocalyptic virus like that from wiping out a population. And most viruses wouldn't kill 100% of the infected.

So what the hell was this?

I shiver, even though the mess hall is hotter than a furnace. Venice likes the heat of the oven.

I look over and see Orion watching me curiously. I meet his gaze straight on, trying to read his expression, if there is anything to his gaze. Do androids think like we do? Do they worry about their own kind of mortality like we do? Is he glad he's immune to biological viruses?

Underneath the table, both my hands make fists, and I concentrate on how different they are. Would I be as frightened as I am right now if I were more robot?

"I think I'm done, too," I say softly, pushing away from the table. "PC, if you want, we can pull out some cards and play poker. I need to do some winning. I have a new leg to buy." And I need to take my mind off Delta going silent.

PC grins up at me. "Sure. See you in thirty?"

I nod. "Anyone else?"

"I'll join," Daisy murmurs.

Taka nods. He's a damn good poker player, mainly because he has a great poker face. At least, when he's mentally present during the game. Sometimes he's off in la-la land with his own thoughts.

"Why the hell not?" Venice mutters. "Maybe I'll have better luck with that instead of my cooking."

If I were a better person, I'd tell him that his food wasn't that bad. But I'm not, and that food was *terrible*, so I just give him a thin-lipped smile, and he raises an eyebrow at my expression.

"I'm in, too," Orion adds suddenly. Everyone else around the table groans. The android looks at them in surprise. "What?"

"You count cards, even when you're not trying," PC says,

tapping his temple. "You're even worse than Taka is. None of us are going to win."

Orion manages to look offended, and I chuckle mirthlessly. "I'll leave you to it," I say, standing. "For now, I need to get the taste of data out of my mouth."

I have to hobble out of the mess hall because my right leg is only working at 63.6% efficiency. I really do need to get a new leg as soon as possible. I can patch it up a little bit more, but there's going to be a point where it falls apart around me. I won't be able to go on downlooting runs with everyone if I'm missing a leg. And I'm the one who downloads the information to her memory banks. We all may be cyborgs to some extent here, but I'm the only one with the tech and measures in place to keep classified information safe.

It's my job to board other ships and steal the information.

I sigh as I near my quarters.

As first mate, my quarters are near Captain Louis's and they're the second largest on the whole ship. Which isn't saying much, I realize, as my door irises open. I've tried sprucing up my room over the years: a few succulents are underneath UV lights in the corner, my lone bunk hugs one wall, and I have a small desk and chair. A small window overlooks the vastness of space beyond. When I was younger, space terrified me, with all of its unexplored corners and mysteries. One could travel the entire galaxy their entire lives and still only see .00001% of all there is in the Milky Way. When you add in other galaxies…

I shudder as I strip out of my work suit and head to my en suite. It's a wet toilet, meaning that the showerhead is over the toilet and I have to straddle the basin in order to wash my hair. With water rations on board, the shower will only go for about three minutes before it's shut off.

What I would give to relax in a bath, like I've seen some Lifers do planetside. I try to imagine what life would be like if I didn't have to worry about water or shitty food or my mechanical body falling apart around me.

It's hard, as this is the only life I've known.

Naked, I stand in front of the mirror, giving myself a once-over. I'm twenty-four years old, with thick brown hair that I usually wear in a ponytail. Most of my face is human—many people, when meeting me, don't even know that I'm really a cyborg until they shake my right hand. My left eye is green while my right eye is mechanical with a metal iris of a matching green color, and I have a few pieces of my brain that are hardwired. Then my torso becomes a mess of both flesh and metal. My left arm and leg are still biological, but the rest…

Well, that's why I'm 52.8% cyborg. Parts of me are falling apart, and I'll need to replace them if I'm going to be useful to anyone. I set my teeth and comb my metal hand through my hair.

"Clementine Jones," I murmur to myself in the mirror, "you are a piece of work." I rub at my head, where a knot is forming where I knocked it on the ship. Hopefully that won't have to turn into a metal plate any time soon.

I hit the button for the shower, and a blast of icy cold water hits me. I shriek a long string of curses together. "Dammit, *Pícara*!" I yell at the ship. "I had it set to hot water! Hot water!"

The temperature increases but only a little bit. I scowl around me.

Captain Louis may not think his ship is alive. But I know it is.

And I think she hates me.

Chapter 4

"Read 'em and weep."

PC sets down his cards. A full house, which far outdoes my three-of-a-kind. Everyone around the mess hall table groans as they all fold. I give him a pointed glare as I throw my cards down. He cackles dramatically as he pulls the holographic chips his way. They aren't really there, only as illusions, but the money he just won is real.

Dammit, that'll set my new leg back by another run or two.

Daisy, Venice, PC, Orion, and I are the only ones playing poker. Captain Louis never joins in our games, and Taka said that he had something in his head that he had to get out. I suspect that, in the morning, there will be marker all over his quarters as he tried to work out some sort of problem. Poor Oliver will have to clean that.

"You cheated," Venice mutters, combing a hand through his bad combover. "You cheated, you bastard."

"Did not!" PC glances at Orion, who has been sitting out of every poker hand. By popular vote, the android is not allowed to play tonight, so he's just been watching our hands as we exchange money, poker chips, and barbs. "Did you see me do any nefarious shit?"

Orion's handsome face pinches, and then his eyes flick to me, as if he senses my eyes on him. A smug smile plays about his lips as he answers. "No, there was no cheating from PC. But Daisy did."

"Lot of good it did me," she mutters, puffing on her vape. Tobacco has been extinct for decades now, so electronic cigarettes are the only things around. Captain Louis hates it, and she never smokes around him, but when it's just the five of us, she has no problem blowing smoke up our asses.

"Aw, poor, beautiful Daisy," PC croons. "You know that cheating never pays off."

Daisy rolls her eyes, muttering a stream of curses under her breath.

I look down at the digital counter for my holographic poker chips. I'm down. By a lot. Maybe I should call it a night. Not that it's never *not* night when you're in space. But the ship's lights flux with artificial light to simulate daylight hours. We may have been born and bred in space, but we're still stuck with the circadian rhythm of old Earth.

I take a swig of Venice's homebrewed moonshine and grimace with a cough. The old man watches me amusedly. "Don't like the grog, Clem?"

"It's pretty foul," I admit through tears in my eye. "I think it fried some of my circuits." My still-human stomach roils as the liquid sloshes around. A warning sensor pops up on my retina, telling me that my blood alcohol content is .007%. That's what happens when you have less than 50% of a body for blood to flow around in.

"I think I'm going to head to bed," I say, clicking off my poker chips. With that, I know that the money PC won from me is deposited from my bank account directly into his, and there's nothing I can do to change it.

I give a small wave of defeat and hobble towards the door. "Night, you assholes."

"Sure you don't want to stay, Clem?" PC asks tauntingly.

"Fuck you, too."

He only laughs as I step through the door, and it closes behind me. I finally let out a sigh, the tightness in my chest loosening. It was stupid to play for as long as I did. It's just that, once I got down by a few chips, I thought I could win it back. After all, Orion wasn't playing tonight, and I thought that maybe...

The door irises open next to me, and Orion ducks through the doorway. I feel my pulse quicken at his stealthy, beautiful frame. "Mind if I join you?" he asks.

I shrug. "You want to hang out with a sore loser?"

"Defeat is such an interesting concept," he muses, sticking his hands in his uniform pockets as we start walking.

"What, they didn't program you to feel shame and guilt?"

"They did not program me to lose."

I laugh softly. "At least they gave you a sense of humor. Venice could use some of that."

He quirks an eyebrow, and if I went just off his face, I can almost believe that he's fully human. "So much of Venice's personality is his angry disposition."

I have to give him that. Trying to imagine Venice Moon with a smile is like trying to imagine a corporation with a soul. It just doesn't happen.

I lick my lips as I look down at my feet. I'm wearing slippers, although the slipper on my right foot is too big. I haven't upgraded my mechanical foot since I was fifteen, so there is a two-size difference between my feet. Most of my parts are hand-me-down or secondhand or cobbled-together by Taka to work somehow.

I'm like a mismatch of different parts. And do I make up a unified whole?

That remains to be seen.

"You know," I murmur softly, "I thought I had a chance to make up some ground tonight."

"How do you mean?" Orion sounds genuinely curious.

I pat my right leg, which is working, but I still have that noticeable limp. "I thought I could win enough of the other's wages so that I could get a new leg. You weren't playing tonight, so I thought…"

He nods sympathetically. "Ah, I see."

"And I blew it."

"At least Daisy still gets her robo-puppy," Orion says amusedly. "Oliver will not be disappointed."

I snort. "She cheated, though."

"Just on that last hand."

Lot of good it did her indeed. I guess I'm glad, though. Oliver truly will enjoy having a puppy running around. And galaxies know that we need to have some more laughter and play around here. We tend to get a little grumpy with each other if we're in deep space too long. We need a vacation and to be planetside for a while. We spend 95% of our time on the *Pícara*, but every once in a while, we go to a planet to remember what it feels like to stand up with real gravity.

I don't know how much more of these metal walls I can take.

We reach my room. "Thanks for walking me back," I say with a small smile.

He inclines his head, giving me a better, more devastating smile. Dammit, I wish he weren't so good-looking. I just find myself mesmerized at times, and I have to blink to bring myself back to reality.

"Have a good night, Clementine Jones," he says blithely as he backs up and walks down the hallway we just came from. "Hopefully your luck holds out in different ways."

I stare after him for a bit before I sigh and open the door. I flop down on my bunk and wince as I have to pick up my right leg and put it on the thin mattress, because there's not enough power to lift it up that high.

"That's so pathetic," I mutter to myself, rubbing my eyes. I have a leg that I can't even lift that high, I have a dull headache from my injury earlier, and I just lost 5 million Space Yen.

I'm such an idiot.

I roll onto my side, facing the wall, wondering if I'll dream tonight. I rarely ever dream, and I've been curious if it's because I'm mostly machine now. Wasn't there a writer on old Earth that asked if robots dreamed? Or something like that.

Does Orion see things when he closes his eyes? That assumes that he ever goes into sleep mode, which I've never seen before, so I doubt it.

I'm settled for only a few minutes when I hear a beep on my mini-tab, alerting me that a message had just come in.

I groan, roll over, and grab the tablet, bringing it close to my face. It's a message from my bank, saying that I've just received 5 million Space Yen. The exact amount I lost in poker tonight. My heart pounds against my metal ribcage as I swipe the screen to see what happened. Did PC feel bad and give me back my money?

I don't think so, because the accompanying message doesn't have his usual snark. Instead, there's a small note that says, "I do not have repairs to make, and I do not require food. This is only fair. -O."

I blink a few times as my right eye starts to burn with unshed tears—the right one doesn't have tear ducts anymore. Orion...*gave* me this money? Why? There are plenty of things that an android could use that money on. He could buy himself from Captain Louis and live a life as he pleased. He could upgrade himself. Or, hell, go on vacation. I know androids feel relaxation to some measure.

Instead, he gave me his sum.

I bite my lip as I look at the total in my bank account. I'm at 43 million Space Yen. Two more runs ought to do it. Two more runs and I should be able to get a new leg. A strangled cry escapes my throat at how close it seems. I hold the mini-tab to my chest and roll on my back, looking up at the ceiling.

"Thank you," I murmur softly. "Thank you."

WE'RE EATING breakfast in the mess hall at 0900 hours when Captain Louis gets an alert that there's an incoming message waiting to be received. His methodical chewing stops as he glances down at his mini-tab, and he scrolls through it.

"PC, Clem, Orion—to the bridge," he says suddenly as he wipes his mouth with his napkin. "Now."

Everyone else pushes away from the table too quickly, even those that weren't called. Breakfast isn't any better than dinner, and based on Venice's hurt expression, he put two and two together that we're all eager for the excuse to get away from our meals.

"What is it?" I ask as I get to my feet. I didn't dream last night, so I either fell into too deep of a sleep or I didn't sleep well at all, but I feel groggy this morning.

"We have another job," Louis says.

I blink. Usually there's a wait time between jobs, lasting anywhere from three to six weeks. We've been known to even go months without hearing from a corporation. So to hear from one the day *after* a job is completely unheard of. We're tired from all the work and planning from the job before.

Still though, a job is a job.

"What is it?" I ask.

"Who knows?" Louis says with a shrug. "But here's the interesting part. It's from Syn-Tech."

I hesitate.

Okay, this is heading into uncharted territory now. Usually the corporation that we literally *just* stole from is mad at us for at least a while before they contact us for a gig, usually in retaliation against their rival company. So if Syn-Tech is contacting us the day after we hit the *Nautilus*, well…

Something just isn't sitting right in my stomach about it.

"Is that wise?" I ask, my voice hitching in my throat.

PC gives me an incredulous look as he walks by me. "It's a *job*, Clem," he exclaims, as if I'm crazy.

I flip him a vulgar gesture before hobbling the rest of the way to the bridge. The *Pícara* isn't a big ship, but the mess hall and the bridge happen to be on opposite ends of the craft, so it is still a bit of a trek, especially with a leg that isn't working properly.

I arrive just in time for Captain Louis to accept the incoming message as everyone else straps in, including Taka, Daisy, and Venice. They're as curious as the rest of us to find out what this job is about. Oliver isn't allowed at these meetings, as there are sometimes some harsh words that are exchanged between us and our prospective employers. I also think that Louis is trying to steer Oliver's moral compass towards not being a space pirate, but I don't see how there could be any other future for the boy.

After all, that's how PC and I became a part of the crew.

Louis manages to look relaxed in his captain's chair as he addresses the screen when it comes on.

I pause in the doorway as I see Chairman Maas fill the frame of the screen. Corporations, due to their secrecy, never let on who their CEOs are, but there is a board of directors that are widely known. Chairman Maas is one of the highest-ranking officials at Syn-Tech.

Usually our jobs are handed to us through minions, the lower-down workers, so that if something is blown out of proportion, these higher-ups can always point to the fact that it was an errant employee that initiated the gig.

I feel everyone in the bridge freeze at the sight of Chairman Maas, including Orion, who must be running a background check on the man. I know because my left retina is feeding me a whole bunch of information and stats about him, from his birth on Synthra, Syn-Tech's planet of operations, to his prestigious schooling, and all the patents in his name.

He's on the same level as God in these respects. And he's talking to the crew of the *Pícara*.

Captain Louis is the first of us to recover. "Chairman Maas," he says, his voice amazingly even. "To what do we owe this pleasure?"

Chairman Maas appears to be in his early thirties, with an immaculate, billion-Yen suit. His blond hair is slicked back, a perfect chiseled jaw, and flawless skin greet us. We can't see his eyes, as they are behind some shaded spectacles, no doubt feeding him diagnostics and background checks on all of us as he regards us.

"You are Captain Louis Stevenson of the *Pícara*, I presume?" he asks, his voice rich and deep, filling up the speakers with his rich baritone. It wouldn't match his unmarred expression if it didn't exude power. As it is, I can see the knot in PC's throat bob up and down.

"I am," Louis says with a curt nod. "And this is my crew."

Chairman Maas sweeps his gaze across all of us, and I can *feel* it when his eyes land on me. An amused smile plays at his lips for the barest moment before he looks back at Louis. "A motley crew of sorts that you have here."

Ordinarily, that would have pissed me off, but at the moment, I'm too scared to breathe. I don't want to piss off Chairman Maas. It's one thing to steal his company's information for pay; it's another to insult him to his face.

So I just stand here, rigid, unable to move.

"They are the best people I have ever known, Your Grace," Louis says thinly. I glance over at him, astonished. Usually, it's hard to ever get a positive word out of him. I know from a lifetime of growing up with him. He's never said he's proud of me, and he only rarely shows affection.

What a day for oddities.

"As they should be," Chairman Maas says placatingly. He smiles again, and a shiver runs down my metal spine. "And if you trust them, then I have a job for you."

"We're on hiatus," Louis says, and I can hear Daisy suck in a breath. She doesn't want to skip out on a job, and I completely understand the sentiment. I may be tired and recovering from being shot, but…a job from the chairman himself?

Maas nods, though, as if in understanding. "Which is why I'm offering you an extremely generous compensation package for accepting this job."

Louis tenses. "You are?"

"How does 300 million Space Yen sound?"

My mechanical lung freezes as I hold my breath, unable to fully comprehend the amount of money that Chairman Maas just threw out. *300 million Space Yen?* Usually runs are between 10 and 50 million Yen, with the rare occasion of going over it. But 300 million is enough to keep us from doing runs all year. It's enough for me to replace my leg and then some.

It's enough to even buy a new ship if we wanted. No more cold showers from the *Pícara*.

Then again, there's usually a reason for that kind of a reward.

"Sounds like a dangerous job," Louis says, echoing my thoughts.

Chairman Maas shrugs. "Only that you would be headed to an abandoned jetter that's drifting towards a black hole."

Louis raises an eyebrow. "Abandoned why?"

Maas nods to a tech behind him, and a holographic map replaces him, showing the area in space where the ship is shown floating towards the event horizon of a supermassive blackhole about 140 lightyears away from our own coordinates.

"Equipment failure," Maas narrates, and the map zooms farther out to show an asteroid belt. "What you see is the *STS Nova*, your target. They were hit by an onslaught of asteroids that killed their navigational systems, leaving them crippled. The crew was able to leave, but they neglected to bring back one last thing. And I—we—*Syn-Tech* needs that information. We could care less about the rest of the ship."

I cross my arms and cock my hip. Something doesn't sit right with me as I look at the map, like my robotic gut is in overdrive and churning up what I ate of this morning's breakfast. But still, 300 million Yen to board a crippled, *abandoned* ship? It's like taking nuts and bolts from a brand-new android.

Super easy.

"I'm sure someone on your crew has already figured out that you have to make it to the *Nova* fairly soon before the ship reaches the event horizon of the black hole and is sucked away forever."

"Orion, is it doable?" Louis mutters to the android.

The navigator nods. "It requires thirty-seven hours in FTL. If we leave now, we will have twelve hours to retrieve the package."

So, plenty of time to make the run. I've made them in thirty minutes before.

"The only other caveat is that you'd have to personally bring the data to me on Alpha," Maas continues. "Within thirty-eight hours of retrieving the information."

"Why?" Louis demands as we're all taken aback by this new information. "We have the most secure uplinks and—"

Maas shakes his head. "This information is of utmost importance to my company, Captain. I can't risk having it intercepted by Varvis-5 or any of the others." He grimaces, his teeth on edge. I wonder what information could be so important to him that he doesn't trust an uplink.

Then again, for 300 million Yen…

"And you have my word that my people will not arrest or come after you. This isn't some sort of conspiracy to capture your crew, so you can lay that to rest. And other than that little added task," Maas says, "it would be the easiest job you've undergone."

"What is it?"

Maas frowns at Louis's direct question. "Come again?"

"What is it that you want us to retrieve for you?"

"Patents," the Chairman says icily. "Extremely valuable patents that my company has not yet catalogued. These are the only copies of them in existence, and if the *Nova* goes into that blackhole, then we stand to lose them forever."

Patents. That sounds innocuous enough.

Louis doesn't show any curiosity towards this new information. "Why the high price if it's all so easy, then? And for patents?"

Maas comes back into frame and steeples his fingers as he scrutinizes Louis. "I'm giving you the 300 million Yen for your time to personally deliver my information to me. And for your discretion. I've been burned in the past by space pirates like you."

"Like us, but *not* us," PC says, speaking out of turn, and Louis shoots him a disapproving look.

To our surprise, Chairman Maas chuckles, his voice a deep rumble that I can feel in my bones and pistons. "Which is exactly why I'm hiring you," he says. "I'm hiring you for your discretion. I know you just fulfilled a run for one of my, ah, *competitors*. But trust me, there's no hard feelings. Not after you got in and got out without harming any of the crew *and* you left before my fighter arrived while sustaining only light injuries yourself."

I bristle at being singled out, and I shift my weight to my left leg so he doesn't see that my right isn't working very well.

With 300 million Space Yen, I could… Stars, I could do so much. We *all* could.

I glance up at the second level where I see Oliver peering down at us, his eyes wide as he listens to us. I narrow my eyes, willing him to stay silent. He's probably dreaming up all of the robo-pups Daisy could buy for him. Maybe Taka could get that horse simulation.

It's a life-changing amount of money. We wouldn't be filthy rich for the rest of our lives, but it would let us get ahead, at least for a while. And that's more than most get in their lifetimes.

I decide that we have to do it.

It may not be as easy as Chairman Maas would lead us to believe, but…we've gotten into some worse situations, and even if I have my other kidney shot out, I could pay for a brand new one.

It's worth it.

"I'm waiting for confirmation, Captain Louis," Maas says.

I can sense that all our attentions are on Louis as he strokes the whiskers of his chin, considering the offer. PC looks like he's about to explode out of his chair and pummel the man's face in if he doesn't accept the job.

Finally, Louis's gaze turns to me, and something flickers across his face before he closes his eyes, almost painfully.

"We'll consider it and get back to you by 0600 hours," he says. "Expect my call then."

A slow, almost devious smile comes to Maas's face. "I'll be waiting for it, Captain."

Then the screen goes blank.

And everyone scrambles out of their chairs to approach the captain, flabbergasted at his decision.

"What the bloody hell are you thinking?" PC thunders, his face turning red with anger. "You're going to wait to make a decision about whether or not you want to pick up 300 million Space Yen?"

"Insubordination," Louis tell him calmly. "And it's not 'picking up 300 million Space Yen,' as you said, PC. There's something else going on here. And I don't like it."

He looks over at me and Orion while his jaw clenches. "Can I have a word with you two?" he says. "*Alone?*"

Now I know he's nervous about the mission. A shiver moves down my spine. And I can't help the sense of dread that's settled in my core.

But still, 300 million Yen? How could he even think about turning that down?

And based on everyone else's expressions, they're wondering the same thing, too.

Chapter 5

The rest of the crew blinks in disbelief at being excluded from this part of the discussion. Usually they're invited to take part in everything, as this is a crew and we're working together. I see the hurt on Daisy's face as she shakes her head and walks past Louis. Taka won't meet his eyes, and Venice seems like he's withdrawn into himself.

Only PC still seems angry as he kicks Louis's console before striding by.

I open my mouth to reprimand him, but Louis shakes his head. "It's fine," he mutters under his breath. "Let him vent. Because this is a private conversation that's important. Do you hear me, Oliver?" he asks, raising his voice. I hear the scuttle of the boy on the second floor, followed by the snick of a door closing behind him.

Now, the three of us are truly alone.

I sigh and rub my temples. "That's…unexpected," I murmur mildly. "I would have thought that you'd jump at the chance, Captain."

"I don't trust him," Louis grumbles, bracing his hands on the captain's console. Like me, he has a prosthetic for one hand, an older model that is rusting from years of neglect. Good thing he takes care of the *Pícara* better than he takes care of himself. We'd rattle to pieces every time we went into FTL.

"I don't trust him, either," I say, trying to appeal to his senses, "but for 300 million Yen, I'm pretty much willing to do anything."

"Orion, what do you think?" he asks the android. "Did your sensors pick up anything…*sinister* in his mannerisms?"

Orion frowns at me for a moment before he straightens and faces the captain. "It is hard to discern his mannerisms and physiological changes over a video call, sir. If I were in the same room, then I could—"

Louis waves his hand dismissively. "I understand that. But —based on what you saw and Maas's track record for being a scoundrel—do you think he was being forthcoming about the job?"

There's a moment's hesitation from Orion as he scrolls through Maas's background once again. I'm doing the same thing, through a different lens than what I searched earlier. Now I'm looking for anything that looks nefarious in relation to spacecraft and pirates.

I find a few things that would make my toes curl in relation to labor camps and what they do to Lifers who try to escape the clutches of their organizations, but otherwise, Syn-Tech keeps their machinations under tight wraps.

"I can find nothing, sir," Orion says.

Louis sighs and ruffles his crew-cut hair, deep in thought. "Clementine, do you think this has anything to do with Delta?"

"The spaceport that the Feds are nuking?" I ask, feeling something biological twist inside me at the thought of all those lives lost. I mull it over for a moment before shaking my head. "I don't know. I don't think so."

"The *STS Nova* is over 780 lightyears away from the spaceport," Orion cuts in. "The probability that the two have anything to do with each other is low."

"But you admit that there's a possibility," Louis says, his voice bitter. Orion doesn't have anything to say against that—it's not in his programming to lie outright, so he can't say otherwise.

"There is one way of knowing," I say a little too excitedly as I stride over to my console, my right leg dragging behind me. "We have the coordinates from yesterday's run."

"I thought you would have purged that by now, Clem," Louis says, his voice laced with disapproval that I broke one of his rules.

"I know, I know," I say as I call out the hub on my right hand. My middle finger transforms, and I plug it into the port. "But after getting shot yesterday, I got so, so tired, and I didn't feel like deleting terabytes of files, Louis. I was going to do it today, but—this just seems like a good opportunity."

I turn away from his deepening frown to look at the screen. My left hands flies across my keyboard, running a search under "/cordinates" for anything related to the *STS Nova*. I pull up a map similar to the one that Chairman Maas had shown us, but this one shows all of the flightpaths the ship has taken in the last six months.

I sit back with a satisfied nod. "The *Nova's* last stop was the Syn-Tech Port Alpha as of three weeks ago," I say, naming the largest, most important spaceport to Syn-Tech. It's in permanent orbit around the planet Synthra, homebase to all of Syn-Tech. It also happens to be in an entirely different arm of the Milky Way from Delta, putting vast swaths of distances between them. There's no way that the *Nova* was at Delta in any way. And based on the rest of the ship's history, the *Nova* hasn't been to Delta in years.

It's simply impossible for the ship to have been anywhere near that death trap.

I look back at Louis. "It looks safe to me," I prompt.

The old man shakes his head. "I just don't know, Clem," he whispers.

I lick my lips. "It's 300 million Space Yen. Do you know what that kind of money could do for us?"

He meets my eyes. "Of course I do."

"And it's not like we're even going against another company's ship," I say, pointing to the screen. "We're hired by SynTech to retrieve information from one of their own. So we don't have to worry about fighters showing up and firing on our asses—we're already on their side."

Louis chews on the inside of his cheek—something that I know he does when he's deep in thought. We almost have his approval. Just a little further…

"Orion, with this new set of information, what do you think?" he asks, grasping for one last bit of resistance.

The android doesn't help him. "It does seem like an easy mission. The crew has done far more dangerous missions for far less. Even with the added timeline of delivering it to the Chairman in person."

"Yes, but I feel like I had a handle on it." Louis purses his lips together, deep in thought. "This feels…sinister. Like he's keeping something from us."

I clear my throat. "We can put extra security measures in place. We'll set the zappers to kill. And I'll have a few more firewalls in case there's malware in the information I'm downlooting. We can handle this, Captain."

Louis narrows his eyes at me, really sizing me up and down, as if debating if I'm able to follow through or not with my proposal. I'm 100% confident. And based on the information my computer's relaying to me, we have 97.4% chance of success. The highest odds we've ever had.

It's stupid *not* to take it.

"All right, fine. But this is *your* mission, Clementine," he says, wagging his finger at me. "I'll put the crew in your charge, and you're the one responsible for getting them out safely."

My inside thermal temperature spikes, coloring my cheeks, and I give a solemn nod. "Will do, sir."

"Don't make me regret it," Louis grumbles under his breath as he pushes a button on his console. The door to the bridge opens, revealing all of the crew huddling around the door to try and get any information out of our conversation. I know for a fact that all of the doors are sound-proof, making it impossible for them to listen in on us.

Still, can't blame them for trying.

"We're doing the run," Louis says, and they burst into cheers. Actual cheers that breathe life back into a crew that hasn't been planetside for months now. It's reinvigorating when we were getting tired of deep space. "And shut up while I'm on the com with Maas," he adds, glaring at PC as my surrogate brother takes his seat once again.

Even though we're calling back way too soon, Maas is still seated and waiting for us when Louis pulls him up on the big screen once again.

"Your Grace," Louis says, as if he expected to have Maas waiting for us, "we'll take the job."

Chapter 6

"Excellent," Maas says a little too cheerily. "I knew you'd come around. You are no fool, Captain."

Louis doesn't look very happy about the chairman's reaction, and I wish he'd wipe the sour expression from his face before Maas changes his mind about hiring us. "Well, money talks, doesn't it?" is all he says.

"It does indeed," Maas says without skipping a beat. "I'll upload the finalized brief to your ship now. I expect the next time I hear from you to be in person within the week. There's no need to wish you luck, so I will see you then."

And just like that, the screen goes blank as the Chairman cuts off communication with the *Pícara*. Louis swears under his breath and simply looks as if he swallowed a rotten space slug. "I don't like this," he mutters under his breath. "Don't like this one bit."

Meanwhile, I can't keep the smile from my face. I'm leading this run, something that Louis has never let me do before. I've been with him since I was a child, watching him lead the various crew members over the years on different runs.

I know that he's been grooming me to take over the *Pícara* when he retires.

Maybe this is the first test to see how I'll do. And his portion out of that payment will go a long ways towards his retirement.

My console beeps as the brief is fed through to our ship. I accept the package and scroll through it as it extracts. Plans for the *Nova*, a manifest, all known activity in the area—what Syn-Tech gave us is a treasure trove. I haven't realized how little we've had to go on in the past until now. Usually, when a corporation is going after a competitor, they have vague schematics and maybe an idea of where the target is located in the galaxy. As it's one of their own, they know everything about it.

Really, this is going to be the easiest job ever. And I'll be able to get my new leg.

"PC, Daisy, and Taka," Louis says, his voice gruff like he needs to drink some water, "Clem is heading up this run. She'll be your leader and your point man. What she says goes. Treat her like you'd treat me on missions."

"So completely ignore her, then?" PC quips, causing another glare from our surrogate father. "Can do, pops."

"I'll send everyone the brief," I say, flicking the folder over to their individual avatars. "Be sure to read it from beginning to end. Just because it's easy doesn't mean that we need to let our guard down."

"But it *is* really easy." PC is already looking through the files before I can stand. "Basically, a proverbial milk run."

"I don't know what that is," Taka muses softly as he scrolls through his own data on his mini-tab. "But I assume it's as easy as this looks?" He indicates the schematics of the *Nova*.

"Don't get cocky," Daisy mutters. "Cocky's when you get killed."

PC snickers as I get to my feet, swaying softly as the gears and wires in my leg adjust to standing. "Orion, set course for the *Nova*. Try to get us there in ample time, in case there are any projections that are off about the strength of that blackhole." The android's face is pensive as he nods. I hope he doesn't have remorse about not agreeing with the captain more. Remorse is impossible in an android—they simply agree or disagree with their programming. Then again, Orion's always been a bit *different*. Like the *Pícara*.

Maybe he just doesn't like receiving orders from me.

"I shall run the diagnostics for the most direct course," Orion says. "I will alert you once we are ready to enter FTL."

I nod. That should give me a little bit of time to work out the kinks in my own programming. "Taka, I could use your help," I say, curling my finger towards him. He looks over at me, curious. "I'm going to need some help putting up some firewalls in my data banks." I'm a great hacker myself, but if Taka and I combine forces, we can put up something impenetrable by any virus.

The engineer blinks dazedly. "Why the need for more?"

I tilt my head to Louis so he knows this is for him. "I'm trying to avoid being cocky."

"WHY DO you think he turned it down in the first place?" PC asks, idly tossing a red ball and catching it. The ball floats to meet his hand, a sign of the *Pícara's* weaker gravity. Planetside, it would fall much quicker. I can't help but be hypnotized by the motion, even as Taka works on his mini-tab, which is plugged into my right arm.

"I think he believes it's too good to be true," I tell him blithely.

"Well, it *is*," PC admits. "But that doesn't mean that it's not true."

"I'm not sure that's how that saying works," Taka says as he quickly types along the screen. After working with him for a little over an hour, I can see how the engineer is even more brilliant than I give him credit for. He approaches code like a virus, trying to find ways to break it. I thought I was good—within five minutes, he had already come up with ways that something malicious could break through. I've only had a little trouble in the past, but now that I see how he works, I'm glad that he's helping me out.

It will make future runs easier on me, too.

"He's just trying to protect us, PC," I say empathetically. "His concerns are for the crew."

PC tosses the ball up and down, deep in thought. "I know that, but…shit, Clem, it's 300 million Space Yen."

"I know. And we're doing it, aren't we?"

A small grin plays at his lips. "I guess that's true. Can you imagine?" He sighs. "After we collect, I'm going to take a loooong vacation on Pan Sun Werks." Pan Sun is another company, known for their advanced gravity systems and Earth-replicating products. Their planet base is a vacation hotspot for all tourists—if they have enough Yen.

"Well, you'll be laying on a beach soon," I say. I jolt suddenly and grimace as Taka gives an apologetic chuckle.

"Sorry," he mutters, though there's amusement in his voice. "Didn't think that would do anything to harm you."

I scratch at my collarbone with my left hand where the metal of my prosthesis meets my flesh. It itches from whatever he did. "It felt…strange."

"I rearranged some of your inner components," Taka says, tapping his mini-tab, and I wonder how the hell he did that without actually opening up my arm and poking around in there. "Now there's a physical barrier between your data banks and the rest of your cyborg parts. If there is something malicious, it won't get past your elbow."

I grin. "Nice one, Taka."

"It does require a new process for accessing it, though," he says, and he flicks a packet to me. My retina screen scrolls through the various steps that I now have to use to access my right hand's data banks.

A small price to pay. It really comes down to an extra step for opening up a valve. I've already committed the changes to memory, and it will take an extra second of my time. No biggie for peace of mind.

"So *you're* running this, eh?" PC says, and I hear a sour note in his voice, causing me to look up at him.

"What do you want me to say?" I ask with a helpless shrug. "I'm first mate, PC. Do you think he was going to do these runs forever?"

His expression falls. "No, I just—"

"We'll talk about it after this run," I tell him. "Just…let him get used to the idea that he needs to let go of a little of his control and then we can see about you getting more responsibility. It'll just take him some time."

"I know, but…" PC pauses and gives me a hard look. "Why you instead of me? I mean, we found him at the same time, so how did you get ahead?"

"Well, for one, I don't interrupt him when he's speaking to a chairman."

He snorts and shakes his head.

"And I'm more responsible than you."

PC bares his teeth. "Are not!"

"Oh yeah." I nod. "Remember what happened at that bar when we were all planetside? You still have a dent in your head plate from that big guy."

"Hey, he was the one who started it!"

I roll my eyes, and I'm so glad that my mechanical eye is advanced enough to follow the movement. "And we had to pick you up from the Feds' jail cell. That left a great impression on Louis, let me tell you."

"You're the one who always gets shot during runs."

I level him with my gaze. "Yeah, trying to protect you guys." I pat my leg. "This last one, I stepped out in front of you, because there's more machine to me than you. And I knew that I could handle it."

That shuts him up, at least for now. "I suppose you have a point then. Since you always know what's best," he says softly before turning on his heel and leaving my room.

I watch him go, frowning after him. There's always been this rift between us, ever since Louis found us years ago on Dark Horse-1, a cobbled-together spaceport that's only accessible to Free Agents. And the best way to tell a Free Agent is if they have cyborg parts.

I have little memory of life before Dark Horse-1. I was just one of the vagrant children on the street with old cyborg pieces holding me together. I remember I was missing my right eye at that point, and my child-cyborg parts were much smaller. I only had the name "Clementine," the only thing I owned. PC found me first and took me under his wing, standing up to the other kids in the slums when they tried picking on the too-small, too-frail girl.

It was that way for a few months. Just life in the dark alleys, digging through dumpsters to see what even the food recyclers deemed as inedible, sleeping under trash. My stomach was biological then, and I remember the constant hunger. PC would always give me some of his scraps and didn't protest when I cuddled up next to him at night.

We were like brother and sister. And when Captain Louis was thrown out of the brothel across the street—even to this day, I don't know what he was doing there or why he got thrown out, because he hasn't been to one since—he saw us, two shivering children.

And for whatever reason, he took us in. The *Pícara* had a different crew back then, and there has been a constant revolving door of downlooters since then. Some gave up the life and decided to go down a different path. Others…well, they just left.

But Louis, PC, and I were the only constants. Even down to Orion. With all his Space Yen saved up over the years, Louis bought Orion a few years back to take the guesswork out of navigating deep space. Eventually Venice, Daisy, Taka, and Oliver made their way onto the ship as well, and we fell into our respective roles.

And for whatever reason, I was named first mate while PC was delegated to boatswain. Even though PC is three years older than me, Captain Louis deemed me to be a better fit as his second-in-command.

I never understood it either, except that PC can be impulsive sometimes. Then again, can't we all?

"Ow," I mutter, the electric shock that zips through my body bringing me back to the present. Taka has moved on from my arm, and he's now poking around the hole in my leg with a soldering iron.

"If you're leading this run, you should do something about this," he says, poking again. I'm prepared for it this time, and I hold my teeth clenched.

"After this run, I'll be able to afford a new one," I tell him.

"Yes, but…this could be dangerous," Taka says. He turns to his tool box and rummages around. "Let me see what I can do about it."

I open my mouth, but Orion's voice comes on over the intercom. "Course has been set for the *STS Nova*," he says, his voice even and measured, sounding every bit like the robot he is. "T-minus five minutes until ignition."

Immediately, my left retina shows a red timer, counting

down the milliseconds until we need to get to the bridge and get strapped into our seats.

I give Taka an apologetic look. "Looks like I'll have to take a raincheck on that. Let's get to the bridge."

He appears to be disappointed as he packs up his equipment, and I feel a tinge of sympathy for him. I can imagine that he'd love nothing more than to open all of me up and see how my biological parts interact with the mechanical ones. Trust me, I do too.

Another time, maybe.

We'll all get to play after this run.

Chapter 7

I stare at the plans for the *STS Nova* for the twenty-eighth time —I know, because my data banks are keeping score with how many times I've looked through them. I just want to be absolutely certain of where everything is on the ship and commit the schematics to memory—the human part of my brain.

It's after 0000 hours, and everyone is asleep, ready for the mission tomorrow. Everyone except me, because I *can't* sleep, not with it looming over my head like this.

I've been over everything multiple times, trying to account for all possibilities and anything that could go wrong. I know where on the ship I'm supposed to downloot the patents for Syn-Tech, I know how many steps it takes to get from the server to the airlock, and I know where I can access backups of the information. It's all there. It's all for me to figure out.

It's not just because Louis has put me in charge of the run; it's because I have the crew's lives riding on me, and I don't want to let them down. I *can't* let down them. I don't think I'll be able to handle it otherwise. There's always an element of risk with these runs, and this one seems to be easier than ever, but...

They're depending on me.

"Your data banks must have stored those schematics even when you downloaded the brief. Why are you insisting on looking at them so much?"

I look up to see Orion peering over at my station on the bridge. His hands are in his pockets again, his unnatural eyes watching me curiously. Embarrassed, I lick my lips and swipe my screen away to my desktop, a photo from a beach on old Earth.

"I wanted to memorize it," I say. "You know, in case my computer brain fails me."

He cocks his head. "No, I do not know."

Self-consciously, I tug at my ponytail, wondering if I'd insult the android by saying that I don't trust my computer brain. Then I wonder why I'm so worried about offending a robot. That's all he is, right? I need to stop thinking about him as a man. I need to stop thinking about him as a *him*.

So I charge forward. "Let's say something gets fried up there—I just want to make sure that I've done everything to make sure that no one gets killed."

"Why do you think your processor would get destroyed?" He sounds genuinely interested.

"Murphy's Law."

"Who is Murphy?"

I blink for a moment before chuckling, passing my left hand over my face. "I don't even know. It's an expression—an *old* one. I think he was a guy from Earth way back when. But anyways, it means that what *can* go wrong *will* go wrong."

His eyebrows pinch together. "If you think this mission will go wrong, Clementine, then you should pull out of the agreement."

"No, it's not going to go wrong. It's just that—" I grasp at what to say, because in a way, he's right. If I truly believed someone would die, I should call off the job. 300 million Space

Yen isn't worth our lives. "I think it's just my paranoia is getting to me. I don't want to fail Captain Louis. Or the rest of the *Picara*."

As if in answer, the ship groans around us.

Orion pointedly ignores it. "It is a very human reaction to believe that the worst will happen. Up until recently, humans only had one incarnation of their bodies. If they lost a limb, it would be gone for the rest of their lives."

The fingers of my cyborg hand twitch in reply, reminding me that my body has been through some trauma, even if I can't remember it.

"Besides," Orion continues, striding to me, "we currently have a 97.6% chance of success with this mission."

"It was 97.4% earlier," I say, confused.

He flashes a devastating grin. "It went up. I found a route to the *STS Nova* that gets us there thirty-seven minutes earlier than initially planned, so that tips the scales in your favor."

I nod distractedly. "That's good. I just—"

"You care," Orion says. He glances at the screen, where our estimated time of arrival is less than seven hours. "And you should rest. At this rate, staying up any later will be a detriment to your mission as you will be too tired to think clearly."

I nod with a sigh. "You're right."

"I am an android programmed to calculate the best way to proceed. I'm always right."

I watch him for a moment, wondering what's happening in that head of his. He's obviously not as nervous as I am about tomorrow. To him, tomorrow is just another set of probabilities and odds, a trajectory that is always changing and needs to be recalculated. On a base level, it doesn't matter to him who comes out alive or not, possibly not even his own survival, because he can just be remade.

Still though, I can't help the thrill that runs through me as he pats my left shoulder. For an android, his hand is softer than my own cyborg parts. You wouldn't know he wasn't human with your first encounter.

"Just make sure that we keep that head start," I say, swallowing back the lump in my throat. "I'd hate to wake up and realize that we took a wrong turn at Albuquerque."

"What is—"

I wave off his question as I stand. "It's another expression, and that one I don't know where it came from. But it's something you say to mean, well, that we ended up where we're not supposed to be."

He frowns. "We are on the correct course."

"Forget I said anything," I say. At the exit, I stop and turn back to him, fascinated at his silhouette as he stands in front of a kaleidoscope of stars streaking past us. He cuts an intimidating figure, and I wish I were more artistic so I could draw this version of him. He looks like a work of art.

He realizes I stopped and looks at me again, his expression unreadable. *Of course it would be. He's an android.*

"Thank you, by the way," I say finally.

"For what?"

"For sending me some money the other night," I say. "You didn't have to do that, and it helps out so much, and with the big payout for this job, maybe I don't need it anymore—"

"I wanted to," he says softly, and I stop blubbering, blinking at him. "I don't need much, and I can't imagine having a hole in my leg." He taps his own right leg, which is in far better condition than most humans. He's corded with manufactured muscle, making him a fine specimen of a man. If he were a man.

"Still, though," I say, trying to fill the silence. "Thank you."

He inclines his head in my direction. "You're welcome, Clementine."

The temperature in my core spikes again, and my cheeks flush red. I turn and walk out before I can say anything else stupid. He's right—I should sleep so that I can be at the peak of mental performance tomorrow.

Everyone's depending on me.

I can't help but take a detour as I head back to my quarters, and I make my way to Captain Louis's quarters. The door is open, weak bluish light spreading across the floor of the hallway.

He's still up.

I give a rap on the doorframe with my mechanical hand, the metal-on-metal clinking sound louder than I expected.

"Enter," comes Captain Louis's voice from within.

I take a deep breath and enter his quarters. Like me, his space is sparsely furnished, although it is markedly bigger. He has a bigger bed than I do, and he has more succulents on the shelves and in the corners of his room, like he's trying to make his own Earth here. I heard a long time ago that humans like to be around nature, which is hard to do because we live in the vacuum of space. Louis was the first to give me my own succulent, telling me that I had my own piece of old Earth with me. Whenever I see them at spaceports now, I snap them up, even though they cut into my water rations.

Good thing they're hardy plants.

Louis is at his desk, and he casts a wary glance in my direction. "Ah, Clementine," he says grimly, "I thought you'd be up."

My mechanical fingers run along the edge of a leaf as I watch him. "Couldn't sleep?"

"No."

"Neither can I."

There's the ghost of a smile on his face. "Orion said that someone was on the bridge. I assume that was you?"

"Yeah. I wanted to remember the *Nova* by heart. In case something happens."

He sighs, the smile broadening. "Good girl. That's why I know you'll make a great captain someday."

My heart twists inside my metal ribcage. So that is why he's having me lead this run. I bite back my initial response, telling him that there is no *Pícara* without him, that I wouldn't able to go on in his stead if he weren't a part of the team. Instead, my mechanical side slips some serotonin which immediately calms me down, and I can sort through my emotions, finding the nugget I need to keep this conversation going.

"I'm afraid of letting you down."

"No, Clementine," Louis say enigmatically, tapping his temple. "You're afraid of letting everyone down. And that's what's going to make you a better leader than me someday."

I cross my arms and lean against the wall. "PC's upset, you know."

A pained expression crosses Louis's face, but he quickly masks it over. "He's too impulsive, too selfish at the moment. He's more concerned about himself, whereas you are more altruistic in your decisions and your reactions. You're what makes a good captain. He's what makes a good secondhand man."

"He won't like hearing that."

Louis chuckles as he turns off the screen to his mini-tab. "Good thing you'll be captain at that point. You can deal with him then."

"When do you think that will be?" I blurt out, but I quickly smooth it over. "Not that I want you to stop being captain, but it's so that I can…prepare."

He shrugs. "Not sure, Clem. I don't want to give up the *Pícara* anytime soon, but I am getting up there in my years. You can't downloot forever, and you'd do well to remember that yourself. The more you do these runs, the bigger the chance of something bad happening."

"That's not comforting, knowing what's happening tomorrow."

He winks at me. "That's why you're going in doubly prepared."

I wring my hands together, thinking about everything. "And if I don't do well tomorrow?"

"Well," he drawls, leaning back, "then I'll have to make different plans. That's the thing with life, though—it never goes in a straight line. You have to keep moving, keep adjusting to make sure you end up where you're supposed to be. Not where you want to be—because you may not even know that yet. But I have faith in you."

"Thank you, Louis," I say softly.

His gaze drifts to the wall where there's a photograph pinned to the wall. It's one of those old-timey ones, actually printed on real paper. It shows Louis, PC, and me at Zona Rica, a corporation's vacation world. We all look much younger, and I barely even recognize myself, with my bright eyes and bubbly demeanor.

"I've raised you and PC since you were children," Louis says, describing my thoughts. "You never owed me anything for it, but I want to say that you two have done me proud. Regardless of what happens, I am proud of you, Clementine." He turns back to me. "I'm proud of the woman you've become."

Woman, not *cyborg*. And the distinction is enough to make me smile at him. "Thank you again."

"Now," Louis says, "I'm sure you're in here because Orion told you to go to bed. And, for once, I agree with him."

I snicker softly. "You know your android too well."

"I programmed him to be pragmatic."

A little too pragmatic at times. And, despite myself, a yawn comes over me, and I cover my mouth with my hand as I let out a little groan.

"And it seems that he was more than right in your case," Louis muses.

"Yeah, yeah," I say, turning to leave. "All right, I'll see you in the morning."

"And, Clem?"

I look back at him.

He opens his mouth to say something—and I suspect that it's three words I've only heard him say once, and that was when I had the meningococcal bacteria so bad, they all thought I was going to die from necrosis. I lost more of my upper arm thanks to that little sickness. But Louis's mouth shuts with a snap, and he only nods at me.

"Good luck tomorrow."

I want to say those words, too, but it doesn't feel appropriate. "Thanks, sir," I say.

And I head back to my quarters, where I lie awake, looking up at the ceiling and wondering how I'll handle being a captain with everyone depending on me 24/7, when I'm freaked out about one mission.

Tomorrow is going to be…interesting…

I just hope I'm ready.

Chapter 8

"Clementine, come to the bridge."

I swim out of an uneasy sleep. No dreams last night, for which I'm glad, as I don't want to have nightmares about the crew dying. I didn't sleep very well, but at least I had nothing lurking in the shadows of my brain, computer or otherwise.

I roll on my back with a groan and rub a palm over my eyes to wipe the sleep away from my left eye. The right eye is already alert and feeding me information, such as the temperature in the room, the humidity, the time, and how much sleep I've had.

At first, I think I just dreamt Orion had called me. Then his voice fills my quarters again, more insistent this time.

"Clementine, please come to the bridge. *Immediately.*"

I glare at the ceiling like he can see me there.

"Why?" I ask. It's 0915, making us at least an hour out from the *STS Nova*. My alarm is set for twenty minutes from now—and I had planned on a breakfast to keep all of us sharp and ready.

So why the hell am I being woken up early?

"We have come out of FTL earlier than planned," Orion tells me. "There is something that you and Captain Louis need to see."

I hesitate. "What is it? Is it life threatening?"

"You have to see it."

So, obviously *not* life threatening, but then what is it?

"Cryptic android," I mutter to myself as I pull on my work clothes that I discarded on the floor from the night before. Laundry day isn't for another few days, so I'm relegated to wearing my clothes more than once. Such is the life of a space pirate.

I pull my hair back into a ponytail and quickly check myself in the mirror. I look like shit. Great way to start today.

I hobble to the bridge, running my fingers along the hallway. No one else is up yet to intercept me, so Orion must have called only Louis and me. Just great.

The door opens to the bridge, revealing that Louis is already there, looking out the window with Orion. The captain's expression is pulled into a deep frown as he looks outside. If I look like shit, he looks even worse. I don't think he got a wink of shut-eye last night.

"What is it?" I call out.

They both whirl to me, as if they had been lost in their thoughts.

Orion is the first to recover. "It is what we do not see."

"What do you mean?"

Orion's fingers fly across the keyboard, and the map that Syn-Tech supplied us for the location of the *STS Nova* is overlaid on the window in front of us, showing a translucent hologram meant to label where we are in the galaxy. I freeze, seeing what is supposed to be there, and I shake my head as it doesn't make sense.

"There's supposed to be an asteroid field here?"

"Yes," Louis says grimly. "This is where the *Nova* was

supposedly crippled by an asteroid. This is supposed to be *why* the ship can't fly on its own."

"That doesn't make sense," I say. "Why isn't it here?"

"I doubt there ever was an asteroid field here," Louis says. He frowns even deeper. "Which means that Maas lied to us. Orion, overlay the flight path for the *Nova*."

A few clicks and an orange streak draws itself right over our own trajectory, showing us that we're on the exact same route the *Nova* had taken. Towards the blackhole.

A strange feeling seizes me. Fear? Or something else.

"What do you make of it?" Louis asks, looking at me.

"I…" I fumble for words. "I don't know."

That's apparently not a good enough answer for him, as his gaze shifts to Orion, who clasps his hands behind his back. "Given the information that Syn-Tech supplied, we are walking into a situation with a great many unknown variables. The odds of success for this trip are currently unknown."

"That's what I thought," Louis grumbles, nearly growling at the map in front of us. "And I don't like it one bit. Who knows what else they've been keeping from us?"

This isn't the first time the crew has been given only half the information for a mission. A downlooter's life is only collateral for a corporation, so a lot of what we have is on a need-to-know basis. This is different, though. This means that something else happened to the ship to cripple it.

"What do you want to do?" I croak to Louis, feeling that 300 million Space Yen slipping through my fingers. There's no way he'll want to go through with this. Not with the odds stacking up against us.

Still though, I reason, *we've been through far worse. And it's 300 million Space Yen.*

"What do *you* want to do?" Louis asks, catching me off guard. "This is your run, Clem."

I glance at Orion, and his expression is blank. No reassurance there. I gulp. But this isn't a decision for one person. "Let's ask the whole crew. This is something they need to weigh in on as well."

Louis's lips pull up in a smile of half-approval.

"And," I say, "we can still veto whichever decision we come to. But we should all talk about it."

"Orion," Louis commands.

The android doesn't wait for the order from the captain. He presses a button for the intercom, relaying it to the entire ship. "All hands on deck," he says. "All hands on deck."

I hope that between the eight of us, we'll be able to find a solution we can all live with. And hopefully not die on a fool's errand.

"SO YOU'RE TELLING ME," Daisy says, pointing at the overlaid map of the bridge, "that there's supposed to be a whole asteroid field here and there isn't? Isn't that a good thing?"

"No," PC mutters, "it means that something else crippled the *Nova*. It means that we don't know exactly what's going on." He scrutinizes me. "Isn't that right, Clem?"

"That's correct." I lean against Louis's console, my arms crossed as I face the entire crew. They all listened to my story with disbelief etched into their faces. I've been mulling it over myself and it doesn't make sense. What could Syn-Tech have gained by lying to us? What are they trying to hide?

Furthermore, what are they wanting us to retrieve from the *Nova*? Should I believe that they still want their patents, when clearly they've lied to us up to this point?

I don't know.

"What if we just contact the chairman?" Taka reasons. "Ask him if he handed us the wrong information."

"No," Louis says gruffly. "The chairman hired us for our discretion, and to contact him before the job is done is to forfeit the job. And I don't want to do that without coming to a conclusion about the risks involved with this job."

"So…what do we do?" Daisy asks.

"It's 300 million Space Yen," Venice reasons. "I mean…" His voice trails off, and we are *all* thinking the same thing.

With that amount of money, are we willing to go through with it? That's precisely why Maas offered so much—so that we *wouldn't* turn it down. Maybe it's reassurance to get us there and finish the job.

That may be giving him too much credit. Then again, he does want something from us—and I'm sure he's completely willing to do whatever it takes to retrieve that information—even if they are just patents. I'm not so sure now.

"What if we continue on our course?" I say. "We have a little over eleven hours until the *Nova* reaches the edge of the blackhole. That gives us plenty of time to get there and assess the situation before we enter it. If we show up and we see something we don't like, we don't follow through with it. If it looks clear—and we'll scan the ship for any malicious activity—we stop and get the fuck out of there."

Granted, that's if we can say no to 300 million Space Yen at that point. Something tells me that the closer we get to the *Nova*, the harder it will be to turn it down.

And maybe that's what Maas wanted.

Louis's jaw clenches as he considers my words. "What does the rest of the crew say?" he asks.

"Aye," PC says immediately, his gaze locked on me.

"Aye," Daisy says.

Venice nods. "Aye."

Taka hesitates, and I can understand why. There are plenty of unknown variables ahead of us, and even if we are all right with boarding the *Nova*, there are still a great many things we won't be able to account for. For someone as analytical as Taka, it would kill him to try to figure it out. "Okay," he says, his voice soft.

"Oliver?" Louis asks.

The boy makes a surprised *eep* as all our attentions focus on him.

"Me?" he asks, confused.

Louis nods. "Yes. You're a part of this crew, Oliver."

Daisy smiles amusedly at the inclusion of the boy. Meanwhile, he looks terrified to have been singled out.

"Clementine, Orion, and I will abstain from the vote if you say aye," Louis prompts.

I exchange glances with Orion, and for once, the android looks unhappy. I focus on it a little too long, wondering what's processing in that head of his, but then I force myself to look back at the cabin boy.

Oliver chews on his bottom lip, as if seeking validation from the rest of the crew. Finally, he nods. "Aye." It comes out as a meek whisper, but it's enough for all of us to hear it.

Louis lets out a shaky breath. "All right. Then we continue to the *Nova*. I suggest you spend this time getting ready. We're going into something we don't quite understand, and I don't want us to get lazy. PC, Daisy, Taka. You're boarding with Clem."

"Aye," PC says. "Will do, Captain."

"Breakfast is nearly ready," Venice says, and we're all so freaked out that no one comments on the state of that breakfast. Venice almost looks relieved about that.

I'm lost in my own thoughts as the crew moves to leave the bridge, getting ready in their own ways for our run. PC passes by me and leans in, whispering in my ear, "Thank you."

I give him a slight nod as he walks through the door. I meet

Orion's gaze, and I notice that muscle is twitching in his cheek again.

"Here's to hoping that we're worried for nothing," Louis mutters to himself, shaking his head. "I'm going to see what that breakfast is about." He pushes himself to his feet, and he heads out as well.

Leaving me alone with Orion.

"You would have said no, wouldn't you?" I ask him point-blank. My pulse is humming in my temples, already giving me a headache. So much for getting some rest and being in peak condition.

Orion is so still, I wonder if he turned himself off rather than speak with me. "Based on the data that I have," he says slowly, "it is inadvisable to proceed with the run. At least until we have further information."

"That's why we're going to run reconnaissance when we get there," I say.

"There are some things that cannot be accounted for, even with reconnaissance."

"That's how they did it for wars on old Earth," I say. "They used to send scouts to see the enemy before making their attack plans."

"And that was back when the average human lived to be thirty-five," Orion quips. "You would think for having a finite amount of life, you would think you would be more careful with it."

I raise an eyebrow. "I think you were being sarcastic just now."

Then, as if to remind me that he's nothing like a human, he doesn't chuckle or react the way a human would. Instead, he only watches me. "Clementine," he says, "my function in this operation is to evaluate risks. And I cannot come to a conclusion at this time."

"We'll come to it together."

He doesn't look convinced. "I hope you are right, Clementine. I hope you are right."

It's later that I realize that he used the abstract concept of "hope."

Chapter 9

Everyone holds their collective breath as Orion pulls the *Pícara* out of FTL. All eyes are on the screen, to be the first to see the state of the *Nova*. I have so many thoughts running through my head, both sides of my brain working in overdrive to guess what we're going to see and what's going to happen next.

I feel the motion of the *Pícara* slow, and the stars stop streaking across the sky.

PC swears under his breath as the situation ahead of us comes into view. Louis is so transfixed by the scene, he doesn't even chide PC for his language.

The first thing I see is the massive curve of the event horizon ahead of us, where even light is captured and sucked into oblivion. I've only been this close to a blackhole a few times in my life, but this blackhole is much larger. It even *feels* more sinister to me, like it's sucking all my hopes, dreams, and even my essence to its core.

It also doesn't match the information that we were supplied by Syn-Tech.

"How wide is that?" I ask in disbelief.

"Three light days," Orion confirms.

My retina computer immediately calculates a comparison to other known blackholes in the galaxy. "So it's almost a supermassive blackhole?" I glance over at Louis. "I thought it was supposed to be a normal one?"

"Apparently, that is another piece of information that Maas kept from us," Louis mutters, putting his hands on his waist. He shakes his head, disapproval evident on his face.

"Are we at the center of the galaxy, then?" Taka asks.

Orion shakes his head. "This blackhole has apparently managed to be hiding from all of us."

Rare but not unheard of. The galaxy and the universe are massive places, and we're still trying to locate and map everything within it. So…it's not out of the realm of possibility that it hasn't been discovered yet.

But it's also true that Syn-Tech could have been keeping it hidden. For what purpose?

"How does that impact our timeline?" I ask, turning to Orion, keeping my thoughts on the subject at hand. "With the bigger blackhole?"

"The event horizon is in the same location on the map that Syn-Tech gave," Orion says. He clacks across his keyboard and gives a small nod at the read-out. "The difference would be negligible."

"We'd just have longer to contemplate death as we're being sucked in," PC mutters.

"Where is the *Nova*?" Daisy asks, leaning in her seat to get a better view. "I don't see it."

"It is here," Orion says, flicking the map onto the window, where I see the red dot indicating the ship. I blink a few times, trying to spot it, even with the dots. Then I do see it. It looks impossibly small compared to the maw that is the black hole. For a panicked moment, I think the schematics I spent so much time trying to memorize are incorrect.

"Can you get us closer to it, Orion?" I ask, my voice hoarse.

Wordlessly, the android flies the *Picara* closer towards that dot. It's disconcerting, seeing the enormous blackhole before us and flying *towards* it, but I swallow my fear as I tell myself so long as we don't cross that line, we'll be fine.

We'll be fine.

The *Nova* grows in size as we near it, and I realize that it isn't as small as I initially thought. It's bigger than the *Picara*, and looking at certain markers, I breathe a sigh of relief that the ship matches the schematics that Maas sent through.

At least that's correct.

Also, I realize that it's in bad shape. It may not have been an asteroid belt, but *something* took chunks out of it, and it looks like it would have fallen apart, even if it hadn't been drifting towards a blackhole.

The computer side of my brain is analyzing all parts of the ship, comparing it with what I've been told and what I actually see. For the most part, it matches. I do know that we're going to have to wear suits and Grav-Boots, as it looks like there's no atmosphere on the craft, and I'm almost certain that the artificial gravity is offline.

The thing looks like a piece of holey synthetic Swiss cheese.

"All the escape pods are still there," Daisy murmurs. "I thought it was crippled and then the crew fled?"

I frown, following where she points. True enough, I see the cluster of pods, all still intact. So, the ship's crew must have had another mode of transportation. Or they're still on the *Nova*. I prepare myself for the possibility of their corpses.

"The dock is destroyed," Taka says suddenly.

"Where?" I demand, glancing over at him.

"Over there." He points at a hole in the underside closest to us. I had dismissed it as another hole, but after having Taka point it out, I see the remains of the dock and airlock.

"Shit," I mutter. Louis glares me, recovered enough from the shock of seeing the blackhole to *now* be disapproving.

"We'll have to spacewalk onto it, then," PC mutters, combing both of his hands though the side of his head that has hair. "There's no other way on it."

Not a deal breaker. We've all spacewalked before, even if it is exposing us to space. We've just never done it so close to a blackhole before.

"Run a scan of surrounding areas and for any life on board," I say to Orion. I doubt there would be anything alive on that ship, but with everything that has happened, I'd rather be cautious than get cocky.

Orion keys in the command for the *Pícara* to run a scan. I hold my breath again, my lungs screaming for more air as I watch the *Nova*. What happened to it? Why does it look like a bunch of asteroids hit it all at once? Or did something else happen?

Were those holes made from zappers? Did someone fire at it to stop it from continuing its journey?

"No lifeforms detected on board," Orion says. There's a tone to his voice that says he doesn't approve, but I ignore it. "And there are no ships within striking distance." He nods to the blackhole. "They must be avoiding the blackhole."

Maybe that will work in our favor.

PC looks back at me. I can tell from his face that he wants to go through with the run. Nothing he's seen has deterred him from that 300 million payout.

And we're running out of time, especially if we have to suit up for a spacewalk.

"What do you think?" I ask the whole crew. "We need to decide."

"I'm for it," PC says immediately, giving me a nod. "I think we came all this way, and there's no immediate danger. We should do it."

The others need a little more convincing, though. Conflict roils on Daisy's face, and Taka is still inspecting the ship, making his own assessment.

"Okay," he says finally. "Okay."

Daisy lets out a breath and then shakes her head. I think she's about to say no when she says, "Two robo-pups, Louis." She holds up two fingers. "I'll do it for two. Oliver needs some interaction."

I glance at Oliver, who doesn't say anything. I think he'll have nightmares about blackholes for a while after this.

I rap on the console and stand. "All right," I say, looking at Louis, "let's suit up. We're running out of time, and I'd like to be out of here before we drift too close toward *that*."

I point at the blackhole, and there's nothing else to be said about it.

We have a deadline ticking in front of us, drawing us ever so close.

And we're about to face whatever's on the *Nova*. Hopefully, it's just space dust and empty hallways. Just grab the patents and leave.

Hopefully, that's all there is to it.

Orion doesn't say anything as he steers us closer to the ship.

Closer to 300 million Space Yen.

Chapter 10

"Spacewalking. Did I ever tell you how much I hate spacewalking?" Daisy grumbles as she shimmies into her too-small spacesuit. Our suits are all a mismatch of different trims and colors, as they are all secondhand. Some of the fabric is so worn, I can see through to steel mesh underneath. One good tear and...

"It'll be fine," I tell her. I cinch the sleeve of my right arm. With no atmosphere on the *Nova*, I'll have to take my glove off in space in order to downloot all the data that Maas wants. I've done it before in the past, but I am starting to get the heebie jeebies thinking about it. "We just go in there, do our thing, then get out. Job done."

"Just how I like my sex," PC says with a grin. "Then again, none of *those* jobs came with a 300 million Space Yen happy ending." He attaches tape to the outside of his jacket. His suit has the worst trouble sealing fully, so he just resorts to taping all the seams. "What?" he asks at my expression.

"Usually, men like to pretend they're awesome at sex," I say. They certainly try to sell themselves that way to me at every spaceport we've been to for the last ten years. At least since I've hit puberty. And the few men that I did sleep with usually didn't live up to their claims.

He shrugs. "I've had no complaints so far."

Hearing that from my surrogate brother makes me cringe, so I just turn my full attention to Taka, who looks like a robot cat tangled up in a bunch of wires. "How are you holding up?"

"I've been better," he says, and I head over to him to help him get into his suit.

"Everyone knows where to go?" I ask as I help him shrug on his outer shell. "And what to do?"

I can't help that nagging question. There's adrenaline pumping through both of my halves, making me itchy and a little sick to my stomach.

"Of course," PC says with a roll of his eyes. "We looked at everything."

"But are you sure—"

"This isn't their first run, Clem," Louis says. "They know what they're doing." He claps PC on the shoulder and gives Daisy a nod. "Orion says we're as close as we're going to get and time's ticking. I told him I'd tell you myself because I knew you'd be freaking out. Am I right?"

He didn't have to ask, but I bite my bottom lip and nod.

"You'll be fine, Clem," he says, giving me a wink. "Just remember to breathe."

Breathe. Right.

Hard to remember to do that properly when you're putting a plastic bubble over your head. My helmet is old and scuffed, and the humidifier no longer works, so my breath constantly fogs up the visor. Not to mention that I can hear my heartbeat in my ears, so loud inside my helmet.

But I lock it in place and give Louis a weak smile. "All right, let's do this."

There's more bravado to my voice than I would have

expected, and it seems to encourage everyone else to get to their feet and twist their helmets on.

"Good luck," Louis says as he gives my shoulder a squeeze. "You'll be fine." He even sounds like he believes it, and I fervently wish he was coming with us. He turns his back and steps out of the airlock, the door snicking shut behind him.

Now it's just the four of us. I give a quick glance around me to make sure that everyone is properly suited up—well, as suited up as you can be with these "suits"—and I face the outer door. There's a window where I can see out to the ruined dock of the *Nova*, so close yet so far away.

I try to not think about how close we are to that supermassive blackhole. *Just get in, get out. Job done.* I had told PC that, but I apparently need to remind myself.

I lick my chapped lips. "We're ready, Orion."

There's a pause on the other end. "Airlock opening," Orion says. I think I'm the only who picks up on the hesitation in his voice, as PC claps his hands together in anticipation.

Just ignore it. Orion is an android and assesses risks for everything. True, there is a big unknown ahead of us, but that's what makes humans different from machine—we can improvise.

Now's not the time to think about how I'm actually more machine than human, though.

The atmosphere is sucked away first so we're not blown out to space when the door opens. Daisy crosses her arms and cocks one hip, her eyes on the window as the door opens. Taka stands stoically, although I can see his lips move as he recites some math problems to himself. And PC is primed and ready to go.

We can do this.

The door opens now, fully exposing us to the outside world. I feel a lump jump into my throat as I realize that the *Nova* is too damn far away. At least it feels that way.

I swallow it down and try to put on a brave face. "Daisy," I command softly, stepping aside as the big woman picks up an old school harpoon gun. Sometimes, we have to go back to old tech to do things quickly and efficiently.

Effortlessly, she aims it at the wide-open dock of the *Nova* and fires, the harpoon shooting through space and zooming right into the hole. She's a perfect shot, and she give a satisfied grunt as she lowers the gun. Taka helps by tying the end off, and just like that, the ship is connected to the *Nova*.

PC gives it a good tug to make sure that it's secure. "Wanna go first, Clem?"

I take a deep breath, and despite my blood pressure being elevated—the readouts on my retina tell me so—I give a nod as I grab the wire.

"Yeah, sure."

I turn off my Grav-Boots, and I immediately feel my feet leave the ground. I fire the thrusters at the end of my boots, and they propel me forward. I don't have to pull myself along or anything, just use it as a guide—because the last thing I want to do is float away without a lifeline. Just a gentle prod with my thrusters and I hold the wire.

Keep breathing, keep breathing.

I pass by the outer edge of the *Pícara's* hull, and then I'm pretty much dangling by myself in space. I make the mistake of looking at the giant blackhole to my right and nearly lose my grip on the wire. Out here, where it's just me and the blackhole, the thing is *massive*, and I feel like all it wants to do is suck me in and spit me out in some wormhole or alternate dimension—scientists never could find out what's on the other side of a blackhole, only that no one's ever returned.

I don't want to try it out for myself.

Still, though, I can almost sense the draining pull of the blackhole.

"Hurry up, Clem!" PC shouts behind me. He's closing in on me since I slowed down to take a look.

Right. I tear my eyes away from the pit and continue my trek across the gap. My retina tells me how far I have to go, and I use it as my countdown to finding solid ground again.

300 meters.

200 meters.

100 meters.

50 meters.

10.

3.

I let out a loud sigh as I enter what remains of the *Nova's* dock. I know the blackhole is still outside, but at least there's some semblance of safety here. I initiate my Grav-Boots again, and I fall to the floor of the dock. As I do so, my retina displays the countdown until the absolute last moment that we can stay on the ship without having to worry about the blackhole. *4 hours and 37 minutes.*

Plenty of time, even with our unscheduled stop at the non-existent asteroid field. We can do this.

I turn on my headlamp and look around. The entire dock has been demolished—we're lucky to even have a place to land here.

PC arrives about a minute later and turns on his own boots. "Well, that was interesting," he says, giving me a big smile.

"I nearly shat my pants," Daisy grumbles as she joins us. "Did you see the size of that blackhole?"

"Wish I hadn't," I tell her, glad that she's at least honest about being scared shitless. I like Daisy. She tells it like it is, and nothing ever sways her from that.

We all turn as Taka joins us, looking a little frightened.

"That blackhole's awful, isn't it?" Daisy asks.

He only nods.

"All right, we're all on board, Orion," I say.

"How's the view over there?" Louis asks.

"Homey," PC says sarcastically. "Maybe we should move in." He gives a look around to punctuate his point, and I roll my eyes.

Just like the exterior, the inside of *Nova's* dock is also decimated. Chunks of metal and debris float around in zero-G. I brush them out of the way. We continue walking, our Grav-Boots making loud clacking noises as they stick to the metal of the floor. The screen for the airlock is dark, meaning that this ship has no power as well.

"Think you can handle that, Taka?" I ask.

"Of course," he says as he opens the panel. Even though he'd been frightened only moments before, having a task to occupy his mind does enough to take away his fear. His fingers are gloved, but they move quickly as he pulls apart wires, threads them together, and sparks some connections. For a moment, the screen on the door is dark. Then...

"Got it," he says.

I give him an excited squeeze on his shoulder. So far so good. "Can you restore power to the rest of the ship?"

He taps on the screen, running through a few diagnostic printouts before giving a noncommittal shrug. "I'll have no problem tapping into the auxiliary power, but it looks like the primary is all offline."

"That's all we need," I say.

He nods and taps the screen a few times. I glance over at PC and Daisy, who both look ill at ease. Sometimes, this part is the most painful—waiting to see what's on the other side of the door.

"Can you check for other life forms?" I ask, my voice hoarse.

Daisy frowns, confused. "Orion already ran a check."

I nod. "I know. But things are different once you're on the ship, and you can't be too careful."

A few more button pushes from Taka, and he says, "None on the ship. They must have fled when the *Nova* was crippled."

"What crippled it if it wasn't an asteroid belt?" PC asks.

Taka shakes his head. "It doesn't say. As I said, we're only on auxiliary, so I can't access the mainframe."

So we'll have to worry about that once we get to the bridge. I'll need to be able to have some computer control in order to access the *Nova's* records and downloot them. One step at a time. And as the door whooshes open, I let out a breath of relief.

"Nice," I say as I motion everyone to start walking into the main part of the ship. "Let's go."

Daisy gestures for Taka to take the lead, but I see her draw her zapper, at the ready for anything to come our way from the rear.

I do the same and take point. Oh, and try to act like I'm not terrified, as I remind myself. It's harder than it looks, but I manage all right with PC at my right. We all have our zappers out, ready in case shit hits the proverbial fan.

"How is it looking over there?" Captain Louis asks.

"Fine so far," I say. "Just moving down the main corridor towards the bridge."

"Is the hull breached everywhere on the ship?"

I look towards the other wall of the ship and see through a hole to space. "Yep. There's nothing airtight about the *Nova* anymore."

"You know," PC says, "on old Earth, there was a language called 'Espanol.' And in 'Espanol,' 'nova' meant 'no-go.'"

"How the hell do you know that?" Daisy asks.

PC gives her his most dashing grin. "I can't spend all my time satisfying the ladies."

"Pig," Daisy mutters under her breath.

"What?"

Banter is a good sign. It means that we're comfortable enough in our surroundings to take our attention off the stress—at least for the moment. I don't join in, as my eyes constantly dart from one area to another, looking for any sign of something amiss. Aside from the chunks taken out of the hull, the *Nova* looked to be a good, modern ship. Syn-Tech sure knows how to take care of their employees. I notice some details, such as frequent, recessed lighting and concealed seams that make the *Pícara* look like a piece of junk.

"According to the maps," I say as I point to my left, "the mess hall is that way, followed by the dormitories."

"We don't have to go down there, do we?" PC asks.

I shake my head. "No." And I don't want to, either. I don't want to see if the crew had time to pack their belongings before they abandoned ship. Nor do I want to see if there are any unfortunate souls who didn't make it to the escape pod.

"Down that hall," I say, crossing another one, "is the way to the bridge. And that one, Popcorn, is the route we *do* have to take."

Everyone falls into line behind me as we hurry down the corridor to the bridge. The entire ship is still, like a coffin. My flashlight illuminates the hallways ahead, particles floating around us like long-forgotten ghosts.

The door to the bridge is sealed, and I curse soundly as we come up to it.

"Nothing I can't handle," Taka says as he crouches to work on the panel. "Just means that there's a firewall to keep the auxiliary power from opening the door. In case of invasion."

"Which is kind of what we're doing, isn't it?" PC asks. I shoot him a look. "What?"

I roll my eyes and focus on Taka working. Focus on it, because there's not much else I can do.

Daisy stands at attention further down the corridor, her

zapper at the ready. There's a tautness to her body, like she's expecting an ambush. "Did you hear that?" she whispers.

My blood runs cold. "What?"

"I didn't hear anything," Taka muses, "because there is no sound in the vacuum of space."

"Okay," Daisy says, sounding unconvinced. "Then did you *feel* that?"

Did I feel something? I stand straight, looking down the hallway where her flashlight is poised. The only thing I feel is the pounding of my heart in my chest, as I hope against hope that there was nothing to feel. Because if that's true, then…

I feel a vibration through the metal of my boots, like a faint *plink, plink*. I look down, wondering if there's something hitting the exterior of the *Nova*. I even lift my foot. I tell my internal computer to try to guess what it is based on the distance and the intensity of the vibration.

The sensation gets stronger, and something in my gut twists, the biological part of me ready to bolt and run. Something's not right.

"Taka," I say in warning. "Hurry."

"Almost done," he says, not picking up the panic in my voice. But PC does, and he frowns my way.

"What is it?" he asks.

"I don't know," I murmur softly. "But I think it means we're not alone on this ship."

"Told you there was something," Daisy says a little too smugly.

The vibrations get stronger and faster. Whatever it is, it's picked up our scent and it's headed straight for us. An android perhaps? Or maybe a crewmember who's wearing such a thick spacesuit, we couldn't pick up his presence. Do metal boots shake a ship that much, though?

Maybe if they tread softly. Still, something in me says that we're not safe here.

"Taka…"

"What?" he snaps, looking up at me.

At just that moment, something turns the corner, and even though there is no sound in space, I swear I can feel the soundwaves as they hit my suit. It's screaming—*loudly*—and it doesn't like us being here.

And I have no fucking clue what it is.

The thing is massive, filling up the corridor. There's no way we can get past it. It has eight spindly metal legs that work mostly in tandem with each other—I can tell that it's not used to walking though, and one of the legs is broken off at the joint and dangles in the air. The structure reminds me of something familiar, but I can't put my finger on it.

That's where the familiarity stops, though, as it looks like there's some sort of organism growing on it, liquid pulsating through large blue veins that run right into the machine base. It's lopsided, with the left larger than the right, and lumpy as fuck. It looks disgusting, and that's the only word that I can think of for it.

And then I see an eye and a mouth on the side, with human-looking square teeth, and I scream. Daisy reacts by firing at the *thing*, catching it on the lumpy side.

"What's going on there!" Louis shouts into the intercom.

PC steps in front of me by Daisy and fires two blasts as well, but the stunning blasts don't seem to faze it at all. "Set it to kill," I say through gritted teeth as I raise my own weapon and pull the switch for the intensity of the blasts. Fuck the rule about not killing anyone—I think this thing means to do us harm.

"Clementine, talk to me!" Louis shouts.

"We found something!" I shout into the mic.

The three of us keep firing at the thing, but it keeps advancing.

"Taka, for the love of galaxies," PC warns, and I can hear the exertion in his voice.

"Got it!" Taka says, getting to his feet. I chance a glance behind us to see the doors open, and I gesture for Daisy to go through, then PC. Taka goes inside first and immediately tears open the panel on that side to work on those inner components to close the door behind us. Hopefully, he can get it closed faster than he opened it.

I increase my firing rate at the risk of overheating my zapper. I can feel the metal of the gun through my gloves, and I wonder if it can melt my space suit.

"Taka!" I shout as the creature advances, obviously not liking us reaching the bridge. "Taka, close the door!"

The lone bloodshot eye on the creature watches me and the mouth opens wide, as it barrels its way towards me. I keep firing, but there's nothing I can do to stop it. I cross the threshold to the bridge, wondering if I should tell my friends to run or hide or get the fuck out.

"There we are," Taka sighs as he taps the screen once. The doors slide shut, but not before I get a good look at the beast as it careens toward us. Then the door is shut, and we all breathe a sigh of relief.

But that doesn't seem to stop the beast. I feel the pound as the beast rams into the metal door, bending it inward. I glance at Taka, and I can tell that he knows there's not much time before it breaches the door.

We don't have very long to retrieve the patents. And I can't help but think that we're running on auxiliary power, which will make it harder to access those records.

We're alive, at least for the moment. Although for how much longer, I have no idea.

Chapter 11

"What the fuck?" PC shouts, giving a vulgar gesture to the door. He thumps his helmet, a sign that the adrenaline is running through him. "What the fuck is that?!"

"I don't know," I say dryly, turning away from the door as the creature pounds into it again. The door bends a little more under the pressure, but it holds. For now.

"You don't know?" he thunders. "You don't know?!"

I level him with my gaze and say icily, "It didn't show up on scanners, it isn't anything I've seen before, and it's outside for the moment. So no, PC, I have no idea what the fuck it is, and standing here to debate that fact is only going to get us killed."

He glares at me but doesn't say anything else. I'll consider that issue closed, at least for now.

"How will we get out of here with that thing blocking us?" Daisy asks.

"There's another exit," I say, a little exasperated that my group has obviously not reviewed the maps as extensively as I have. Then again, when have I ever gone over them with the same fervor that I did this time? I'd always been cocky, thinking that nothing could ever kill us.

I was so goddamn wrong.

"Taka," I say, licking my lips, "help me get the main computer turned on. Daisy and PC, stay at the door and shoot if it comes through."

"You got it," Daisy says, cocking her zapper.

PC presses his lips into a thin line but nods as he faces the door.

Taka seems to be out of sorts as he follows me to the console. The bridge is like many other bridges I've been on, although this one is much bigger than the *Picara's*, with enough room for at least a dozen crew members to sit here. The captain's console is easy to find, so I sit down in the chair and face the console. Like I expected, it's dark with no power running through it.

"Think you can fix that?" I ask. "And quickly?"

"I'll try," Taka says as he kneels at the front of the console and starts pulling stuff out of it.

"Don't try, *do*," I mutter as I take off my right glove. My metallic cyborg hand greets me, and I wriggle my fingers, almost in fascination that it all still works. *If* Taka can connect the power and *if* that happens before the door fails, I'll still have to take some time to search for and downloot the information. If the packet is small, then that shouldn't be a problem.

If it's larger, though, then we could very well be screwed.

"Are you guys all right?" Louis asks, his voice steely.

"For the moment," I answer as I call out the plug from my middle finger. "The door's holding for now."

"What is it?" Orion asks, his voice coming over the speaker in my helmet.

"I don't know," I say, inwardly shuddering at the memory of the creature. "It looked like…a bio-mechanical…*thing*…"

"It was a modified arachni-lift," Daisy adds. "You know, one of the machines they use to unload cargo at the docks."

That's where I'd seen it before. I hadn't put the two together because it seemed so far-fetched that an arachni-lift could end up looking like that.

"What the hell happened to it?" PC asks, echoing my own thoughts.

Daisy throws her hands up in the air. "How the fuck should I know?"

"Guys," I say placatingly, "we'll figure that out later. For now, we just have to get this working."

"This isn't worth 300 million Space Yen," PC mutters under his breath.

"Clementine." I pause at the sound of Orion's voice. "This is just a private line between you, Captain Louis, and me. Mute your microphone."

I press the button. "Okay."

"Clem," Louis says, his voice rough, "should we pull out of this job? Are you in danger of being killed?"

I hesitate and look around at Taka who is trying to power up the console, and at PC and Daisy, who are guarding the door. I think of everyone back on the ship who gave up some hope and time to make it here. Were we fools for thinking that this would have been an easy run? Did we foolishly ignore the signs that this was doomed from the start?

"I don't know," I admit softly.

Another shudder rocks the bridge. I glance back at the door and see PC and Daisy aiming their zappers at it.

Suddenly, the console roars to life, and I nearly sob with relief.

"It's ready," Taka says.

I re-open my coms for everyone to hear. "Good. Now, get *that* door to start working and have it ready for when we need to run." I point the door on the opposite side of the bridge. It connects with the rest of the ship via the dormitories and the mess hall. It looks like we'll be able to see how the crewmembers of the *Nova* lived, although I doubt we'll stay for tea.

I imagine we'll be running the entire way.

I navigate the computer to the documents screen and then insert my finger into the port. A hiss escapes my lips as the shock rocks through me. That had been unexpected. I didn't think that the computer would have that much *zing* as I plugged myself in. I gag, feeling my tongue blister with the electrostatic charge.

"Ow, fuck."

"Sorry," Taka says. "I diverted most of the auxiliary power to that console."

"I noticed," I mutter as I access the computer, tearing down the firewalls with the usual methods. It's a bit harder this time, but it only takes me another couple of seconds to improvise and find a workaround.

I get in.

I inhale sharply as I'm bombarded by an operating system that feels different on my brain and on my circuits. It's a newer format than any of the others that I've been in. The data packets are smaller, and the entire thing is organized differently.

And it feels oddly empty as I poke around.

My brows furrow together as I work.

"What's wrong?" PC asks, noticing my concentration.

"Just a different system than I'm used to," I say. "Nothing to worry about." Then, as if to reinforce my statement, I find the folder name that I'm looking for.

/patents/infinity

Exactly what the brief told me to look for. The file itself is encrypted and behind so many firewalls that I have to run a few hacking programs to even get permissions to copy it. I won't be able to access them, but I don't need to, unless I want to figure out what the hell was so important that Chairman

Maas is willing to pay us a fortune and risk our lives. Not that he cares what happens to us, but this must be a very important piece of information.

Curiosity piques my interest. Then again…

I grimace as the door shakes, even harder this time. The door won't hold much longer. I quickly move the files onto my internal storage system, packing it tightly and safely, and then I unplug.

"Got it," I call out to PC and Daisy as I shove my glove back on. "Let's get the fuck out of here. Taka, how's that door coming?"

"Ready when you are," he says as the door opens.

"All right, let's *move!*" I say, grabbing my zapper and getting to my feet.

Daisy rushes the other door while PC slowly walks backward, his eyes still on the door. It shudders again, and I know that one more good ram, and it will be broken.

I touch him lightly on the shoulder, seemingly breaking him out of his trance. "Run," I say.

We both turn and sprint towards the far end of the room, thirty yards away. Taka is already on the other side, working on that panel to close the door behind us. I *feel* the door behind us burst open, but I don't take the chance to see if the creature is right behind us.

I just keep running.

It isn't until PC and I are on the other side that we turn around to fire shots back at the creature. I scream in anger, shooting at the thing.

It's so damn close, reaching out towards us.

The door shuts, sealing it in the bridge.

"Dammit!" PC curses. "Dammit, dammit, *dammit!*"

"What now?" Daisy asks.

I give her a brave look. "We run to the dock as fast as we can."

She doesn't need to be told twice. For a big woman, she moves surprisingly quick, her shorter legs pumping her massive body along, running faster than I thought possible. Taka follows her, then PC. I take up the rear, shouting directions as we move.

Funny how they didn't know much about the layout of the *Nova* before, but now that our lives depend on it, they're remembering it a lot easier. In many cases, they don't need my directions. I still say them though, since a wrong turn could be our last.

I just keep thinking that if that thing is sentient, if it knows how we're trying to leave, it could try to intercept us at the dock…

Don't think about it.

We round a corner, and, like a dream, the dock is there, still in the same state. No creatures here, just the wire and the harpoon that Daisy shot out. I make a mental note to disconnect ourselves as soon as possible in case the creature gets any ideas.

"Orion, we're coming back onto the *Pícara*. Prepare the airlock for us," I command as I help usher Daisy onto the wire.

"Is it safe?" he asks calmly. "I'm detecting a space-born—"

"Fuck you," PC snarls, not calm himself. "You need to let us get off this hunk of space junk."

"Clementine?" Orion asks.

"It's safe," I say. "We just need to hurry. If the torpedoes on the *Pícara* are working, I suggest we send one to the *Nova* to give it a push towards that blackhole though."

I can only imagine that nightmarish thing swimming its way towards our ship and getting attached to it.

"I will see if that can be accomplished," Orion says. "But I am concerned."

"Do you think that thing is what caused the hull and the dock to be breached?" Louis asks.

"I don't know," I say as I help Taka grab the wires and propel himself towards our ship. "Those holes seem to be a bit too big, even for that."

Louis pauses. "So maybe they were firing *at* the *Nova* because of that creature?"

I hadn't thought of that, and I exchange an uneasy glance with PC. "Possibly?" I admit. "I just want to get out of here."

"Did you get the loot?" Louis asks.

"Yeah." I pat my arm for good measure. "It's all there. So, regardless, we'll get the money."

"It'll be enough to buy holo-therapy," PC mutters as he fires his thrusters to pull himself back to the *Pícara*.

That just leaves me.

"FYI, I'm going to cut the wire, guys," I say, turning off my Grav-Boots again and reaching for the wire.

"Good," Daisy mutters. "Cut that bitch."

As soon as my fingers touch the wire, I see the whole thing quiver, announcing the arrival of something *big*. I look behind me to see the eight-legged monstrosity arrive at the docks.

Shit, shit, shit, shit, I chant as I fire my own thrusters, a little bit too hard. I nearly lose my grip on the wire, but I'm able to hold on as I right my course. Luckily, I have a pair of wire cutters attached to my utility belt and I pull them out and pick a place far behind me so I can cut our tie to the *Nova*.

I look at the creature again. It's standing at the edge of the dock, as if debating whether or not to jump and join us on the wire towards the *Pícara*.

That seals the deal for me. I squeeze the cutters, and immediately feel the slack in the wire as it loses one end. That doesn't make our trek to the *Pícara* any easier, though, as instead of an easy zipline to and from, we now really have to pull ourselves towards it, using our thrusters to aim us in the general direction.

And, just because I'm a masochist like that, I turn my head

and see the blackhole, ever so much closer than before. I gulp, feeling impossibly small compared to it, and use that as an excuse to keep us going. I can't quit now. I have to keep moving.

"Clem, how are you doing back there?" PC asks.

"Fine," I say, averting my eyes from the horrible sucking sensation of the blackhole. "Glad to be off the *Nova*."

"You and me both," he mutters, and I snicker despite myself.

There's something wonderful about cheating death and getting away from something so terrifying as that creature. And with that 300 million Space Yen that Syn-Tech is going to give us, I don't want to do another run for a long time.

I look back at the *Nova* and see the creature is still there, farther away than before. It's just sitting there, like it's watching us. Like it knows that it can't follow us. Hopefully, it will stay that way.

I breathe a sigh of relief as I continue pulling myself along. Now, all I have to do is get to a console and get the fuck out of here.

The 300-meter trek to the *Pícara* is long and hard, especially with adrenaline running through me like a quadruple shot of caffeine. I keep replaying everything in my head, wondering which choices we could have made to have a different ending.

Don't worry about it, Clem. No one died. You got the information. Just get to Alpha, give Maas the info, and collect. Happily ever after.

Right.

With my right hand, I reach out to grab the wire. Only my fingers start to squirm, moving more and more in an erratic pattern. *What the fuck?* I stop and look at it, like it's no longer an extension of myself, like it's something else entirely.

"Clem?" PC asks, looking back at me.

"I…" My breathing becomes labored as I put all my

mental focus into trying to take back control of my hand. Maybe I lost connection with it and it's reacting to other stimuli.

Or—and this is even more likely—I downlooted a virus to myself, because it's that exact hand that I use to connect to the computer. It's where I keep my data; it's where the packet is stored.

Fuck.

I grind my teeth and focus even harder on maintaining control. My fingers move of their own accord, reminding me of space maggots. I move my arm and send a signal to those fingers to grasp the wire.

And my hand reaches one way and then shoots itself across my body with such force, I lose my grip with my left hand, and I tumble away from the wire and the *Pícara*.

Towards the blackhole.

Chapter 12

I scream into my microphone as I tumble away from the safety of the *Pícara* and the wire. My inner gyroscope is spinning, unable to show me which way to orient, and the G-forces on me are enough to keep my left hand from reaching my thrusters.

"Clem!" Louis shouts. "Clem!"

I can't stop screaming, terror filling every part of my being. My cyborg side is telling me that my pulse is thready and I'm breathing too fast, but even though I'm getting doses of serotonin, there's no calming me. Because with no way to right myself and to make it back to the *Pícara*, I'm going to die.

And it doesn't help that my hand won't stop squirming, weaving in weird, erratic patterns that only add to my off-kilter spin.

"Clem, you have to calm down!" Louis says.

"I can't!"

"Calm down, and you'll be fine. You have to stop your spin."

I take too-shallow breaths, and my vision is blacking out. I'm not sure if that's from hyperventilating or my spin that's causing the blood flow to go from my head. I have thrusters. I just need to…

A body slams into mine, causing my trajectory to spin in the other direction, albeit slower. I scream at first, thinking that the creature jumped from the *Nova* and caught me. *I'm going to die, I'm going to die.*

"Relax, Clem. I've got you."

I've never been so happy to hear PC's voice. I sob, clutching at him with my left arm. The other arm is still acting up.

"Relax," he says. "And try to get that arm under control." He reaches down and hits his thrusters. I immediately feel the change in direction as he aims us back towards the *Pícara*. Back towards safety.

"Thank you," I whisper.

"Don't mention it," he says. "This is what we do. We're family."

We're family. I close my eyes, grateful that he's able to help when I couldn't.

The dock to the *Pícara* is open, and PC initially overshoots, then corrects us, and propels us into the inside of the ship, where Taka and Daisy are waiting for us.

"We're in!" he yells as soon as we're inside.

The airlock shuts down, and the artificial gravity is turned on. We both hit the floor, hard, with a groan. I immediately let go of PC and roll on my back, groaning as my arm keeps twitching.

"Hey," Taka says as he pulls off his helmet, "let me have a look at that."

"No, I will."

We all turn to have a look as Captain Louis enters the airlock, wearing a spacesuit himself. Ridiculously, I wonder why, and then it hits me. He's afraid of breathing in the same air as us.

He gestures with his head. "You three go to the quarantine showers. We don't know what that thing is, but if you tracked anything from the *Nova* onto here, we need to sort it."

"But—" PC starts.

"*Now,*" Louis growls. He bends over and drags me to my feet. "Clem, come with me."

He practically drags me from the airlock to a room just off the dock. It's a quarantine room all by itself, where we keep anything that looks suspicious during our travels. I remember we kept a reptile here once that PC brought with him, thinking it could be a pet. We had to eject it when the thing grew to be the size of a full-grown man. And it was mean as hell.

The room is small and empty, as we haven't picked up anything in a while. There's a lone table in the center and a pair of chairs. Not our most high-tech room, but it's hermetically sealed from the rest of the ship.

Does Louis think I'm infected with something?

Louis shuts the door behind us, and I notice that he locks it. And that alone scares me as much as falling into the blackhole.

He seems to pick up on my trepidation. "Let me have a look at your hand," he says. His expression is grim, but his voice is softer than before.

"Louis—"

"*Now*, Clem."

I have to fight with my arm to take off the glove. Seeing my familiar hand move and twitch without me telling it to makes it feel like some sort of alien appendage all its own.

"Do you think you downlooted a virus?" Louis asks.

I blink, taken aback. "I don't know."

"Clem."

"I don't know," I say, exasperated. I force my hand onto the table, and it still twitches and tries to buck me off. "It randomly just started doing this on the way back."

He gives me a hard look. "Don't take off your helmet," he says. "Not until you've hit the quarantine showers."

"Do you think we picked up something?" I ask.

He doesn't answer.

"Louis?"

"Look, all we know is that Orion picked up something on the sensors when that beast appeared."

"What was it?" A pathogen? A space-born virus? Is that why it's headed toward a blackhole?

He shakes his head. "Something…weird. Something different. We don't know. And with your hand acting this way, we don't want to take any chances. So we're going to remove your hand here and leave it in quarantine. Hell, even just give it to Maas. Make him deal with it."

I chew on my bottom lip, and he catches my hesitation. "You can use your old arm, Clem."

The one I changed when I was fourteen years old. It was made out of a more brittle metal and rusted in a few places. But I suppose that's better than going without my arm for the foreseeable future.

I nod. "All right." I'm not happy about it, but it does make sense.

Louis sits down at the chair opposite me and pulls out his toolkit. "You know, when that thing first appeared," he says softly, "I thought we had lost you."

"Me too," I whisper. I keep replaying the scenes in my mind—and it doesn't help that my retina videoed the entire thing. I can access it at any time, and I just keep replaying it over and over again. It's absolutely crazy what happened. How an arachni-lift could suddenly just go…psychotic like that.

"Have you ever seen anything like that before?" I ask.

Louis shakes his head. "Never. But that doesn't mean anything," he adds quickly. "The galaxy is a big place, and maybe it was just a matter of time something like this happened."

"But what *is* this?"

"I don't know. An experiment gone very, very wrong? Aliens? I don't know." He starts prodding at my metal arm, and the entire thing jumps in response. I grunt, holding it down. It's hard to keep my grip on it, because it's fighting me.

"We shouldn't have gone," I say somberly, averting my eyes from Louis. "We should have called it off at the asteroid field."

Louis pauses and sighs. "No, Clem. You went with what you thought was right. You thought you had it under control."

I give a derisive snort. "And it turns out that we had nothing under control."

"Welcome to being in charge," he says grimly. He unlatches a section of my upper arm, and despite the fact that my arm is writhing, I can still feel him working in there to disconnect my arm. "I would have still gone," he adds quietly.

"You would?"

"Yes. We get half-truths from corporations all the time. It's a part of their whole policy of telling us crucial information on a need-to-know basis. I would have thought that this was one of those cases." He chuckles dryly. "Hell, this probably still qualifies as such."

"Orion wouldn't have gone," I admit.

Louis pauses again. "And that's why he's an android and you're a human," he says. "Androids only work in absolutes, Clem. They assess risk, and if the threshold is too high, it's in their nature to not proceed. But as humans…we can go with the flow, as they used to say on old Earth." He nods towards my chest. "You have a human heart. You allow for impossibilities."

"I feel more machine than human sometimes."

"We all do," Louis says. "But you do what's right for the crew, even though you're not programmed to do so. And that makes you have more humanity than anyone else. Chairman Maas may not have any cyborg parts—but he's a cold-hearted machine through and through." He gives me a rare smile. "Remember that."

I nod and force the lump in my throat back. "Okay."

It's rare that Louis and I have heart-to-hearts like this, and we've had two in the past few days. I can't help but feel a sense of dread, like I won't have much longer to spend with him. And I have so many questions I need to ask, so many unspoken words.

But that's not our relationship. So I don't say anything as I just watch him work. Between me holding down my arm and him severing the connections, we make short work of it. Eventually, my fingers stop moving as power is cut off. Gingerly, almost in disbelief, I lessen the pressure. It stays still.

He grins at me. "At least that's over with."

Suddenly, my hand springs to life, turning into its computer hub configuration. We both jump to our feet with surprised shouts as it dangles from my shoulder. That doesn't stop it from weaving its way towards Louis.

And—absurdly—a sharp edge of my middle finger rips through the fabric of the forearm on Louis's spacesuit and digs into the flesh underneath.

Louis throws his head back and screams raggedly.

I recoil in horror. "Louis?" I ask. "Louis?"

He doesn't answer—*can't* answer—his scream just continuing on and on, for longer than he should have had breath for. His entire body seizes up, and he doesn't move, but his breath fogs up the dome of his helmet, and I can't see his face anymore.

Just that incessant screaming.

My arm is still connected to him, and I back up from it, trying to let go of him. Trying to stop him from screaming. It doesn't seem to want to let go, though. I start hitting it, trying to knock it free.

"Louis, I can't help you!"

No answer, other than screams. I put my leg up on the table and push against it with all my weight. I groan with exertion, trying so hard to let go.

What the fuck is happening?

Suddenly, I fall hard on my ass, panting. I try to get to my feet, but I no longer have my right arm attached to me. As if I'm watching a nightmare, I see that it's still connected to Louis. And something is happening to him.

While he's still screaming, he moves for the first time since he got the puncture. He flops over the top of the table, grasping at the edge of the table with his unaffected hand. It scrabbles for purchase, but even when he gets a hold of the edge, he lets go. The other arm just shakes, like he's having some sort of seizure.

I kick myself away from the scene, using my legs to scoot all the way to the wall. What do I do? I can't do anything. *And that screaming just keeps on going.*

"Louis?" I ask, my voice sounding hollow in my own ears over the screaming.

"Clementine, what is happening?" Orion's voice cuts in over the din.

"I—I—" I stumble for words, unable to piece together a coherent thought. "I…"

"Clementine, Captain Louis is screaming, and his vitals are off the charts," Orion says, and his voice grounds me.

"I don't know. My arm pierced him and this happened and —" I'm abruptly cut off as I notice something happening with Louis. His hand comes up and unlocks the helmet and pulls it off.

Now it's my turn to scream.

As the helmet leaves the rest of the spacesuit, red, white,

yellow, and flesh-colored *goop* drips out of the spacesuit and onto the table, coating it. So much thick liquid covers the surface that it drips down the sides, onto the floor. And stays there.

As for Louis's head, I watch as it melts into the table.

No.

No, this can't be real.

This just has to be a bad dream. Right? What a time for my brain to suddenly give me a nightmare.

But I don't wake up. And the thing that was once Louis falls against the table, its knees buckling as that liquid keeps pouring out, bubbling all over the place. Bubbling with thick veins that appear and pulsate.

I recognize what that looks like. Impossibly, I've seen it before.

It looks like the living organism that was on the arachni-lift on the *Nova*. I remember seeing human teeth and an eye. I didn't even consider it had once been human.

I didn't think—for one second—that it would happen to Louis.

The goop streaks its way towards me, and I recoil in horror, getting to my feet. What do I do? How do I stop this?

"Clementine?" Orion asks.

"Something happened to Captain Louis," I whisper.

"What?"

"I—I—"

Then the leg of the table twitches. No, not just twitches. It moves. Towards me. Trying to get at me.

I look at the locked door on the other side of the room, the only way out of the quarantine room. It's my only escape. I'll get to the showers, and then…and then…

The table lurches towards me again, and I swallow back my scream, hoping to not tempt it. How the hell is it moving? It's like what used to be Louis assimilated into the table…

Like whoever was around that arachni-life assimilated into it. Became a part of it. Holy shit.

I lunge for the door, jiggling the doorknob for a moment before I unlock the deadbolt with my one hand. I hear the spindly legs of the table as whatever it is starts walking toward me. I turn the knob and fall out of the room, landing hard on my side. No time to wallow in pain though—I get to my feet and throw my shoulder against the door, shutting it just as the table slams into it.

It hits it again. And again. Unlike the door to the bridge and unlike the mutated arachni-lift, the table doesn't make a dent.

Breathing heavily, I lock the door from this side.

"Orion," I murmur as my adrenaline fades, leaving me feeling empty. The knowledge that Louis died—because of *me* —hits me, and I feel a tear slide down my cheek. "Tell everyone—under *no* circumstance—are they to enter that room."

And, dazedly, I make my way to the quarantine showers. Where everything hits me all at once.

Chapter 13

I sit, crouched in the corner of the shower long after it goes cold. The *Picara*, it seems, is kind enough to give me hot water, at least until we run out. I'm still wearing what remains of my spacesuit, although I left my glove and part of my arm back in the quarantine room with...

With Captain Louis...

My helmet's somewhere in here with me. I took it off after I washed with the isopropanol bath. Now the water is just soaking me underneath my suit as it's pouring down my neck and filling it up. I should have turned off the water a long time ago due to the water rations, but I can't bring myself to do so.

I keep thinking about Louis and what became of him. How what's left of him is still in that room.

PC, Daisy, nor Taka was in the showers when I arrived, which is fine by me. I wouldn't know what to tell them or how to break it to them that our captain is...is...

A sob catches in my throat, and I hug my knees closer to my chest. Oh galaxies, why? Why did it do that to him? Was it some sort of virus? Or something different? What happened to the crew of the *Nova*?

Furthermore, should we still be worried about it spreading?

There's a knock at the front of the stall before the door opens. "Clem, you in here?"

It's PC. He doesn't sound like his cheery, happy self. Instead, there's restraint to his voice, like he's been trying to keep himself from screaming or crying. Amazing how the two are similar.

I open my mouth to answer, but I don't have the words. Instead, I just grimace and turn away.

"You're getting your spacesuit wet," he says finally.

I have visions of the last wet spacesuit I saw—Louis's as his body drained out of the suit and onto the table. I pick at the broken wires and cables on my right arm. "I don't care."

"Yeah, you do," he says. "You should also conserve water. Our filter's getting pretty old, and we waste enough as it is." He palms the shower, and it turns off. With the heat of the water, I start shivering.

I think it's from being cold and not from terror.

"What happened, Clem?" he asks, stepping into the shower, his boots sloshing in the puddles. "I saw the video footage, but—"

"Then you saw all there is to see," I murmur, still not meeting his eyes. "One second, he was talking to me, trying to get my cyborg arm under control, and the next, *that* happened."

"*What* happened?" he asks a little more forcefully. "What happened to Captain Louis?"

I press my lips into a thin line and inhale deeply through my nostrils before leaning my head back with a tired sigh. "He was working on it, and it was nearly disconnected, and then, suddenly, it…it…" I take a breath, steadying myself, because I have to get the words out. "My finger slashed open his suit and stuck him."

PC looks at me in disbelief. "Slashed open his spacesuit?"

I give a mirthless chuckle. "Yeah, it's ridiculous, isn't it? It's supposed to be tougher than that." Then again, we're using old-ass spacesuits anyway, so maybe we were signing our own death warrants. "But, that's what happened." I sigh. "And then you know the rest."

His gaze turns hard, and he sticks his hands in the pockets of his trousers. "So what do we do?"

"What do we do? I don't know. We're a ship without a captain, and we're next to a supermassive blackhole, and our quarantine room has a half-human, half-table in it with the rest of my arm." I tap my head against the steel wall of the shower and shrug helplessly. "I don't know, PC. This feels like rock bottom to me."

PC doesn't answer me, at least not right away. He comes forward and grabs my left arm in a vice-like grip.

"Ow, PC, you're hurting me!"

"You're not allowed to give up," he growls at me. "With Captain Louis out of commission, you're the acting captain. And as the acting captain, you have five other people's lives plus an android's existence in your hands. You're not allowed to give up on them. On us." He shakes me roughly. "You need to pull your shit together and figure this out. I was always jealous that you were first mate. Now prove to me why Louis trusted you that much. Get up."

I meet his eyes, and the vehemence in his voice makes me stop and consider everything. There are people counting on me. Louise entrusted me with this responsibility, I have to follow through with it. Suddenly, the panic that I was feeling bleeds away, and I manage to take a breath for the first time in what feels like forever.

"Okay," I whisper, nodding. "Okay."

"I can let go of your arm now, and you won't lose it?"

I nod. Gingerly, carefully, he lets go of me, and I sink back onto the floor. We stay like that for a few minutes, with him breathing heavily while I'm still contemplating my next move.

Finally, PC taps the side of the shower, his metal hand making clinking noises. "It was awful to see, wasn't it?"

"Yes," I admit. "I'm...going to have nightmares for the rest of my life."

"Well, we need to make sure that you live long enough for that to have meaning. And that means not giving up." He extends a hand out to me. "Are you ready?"

I reach out for his proffered hand, and he pulls me to my feet. I'm weak in my knees, even though they're both metal. I brace myself against the wall and force myself to move. Away, out of the showers. And to face the rest of the crew.

I grit my teeth and keep walking, repeating a mantra to myself. *My name is Clementine Jones, acting captain for the* Pícara. *And I'm not going to let my crew down.*

PC takes my arm more gently this time, and we start to walk together, leaning on each other for support. "I'm sorry," he murmurs into my ear.

"For what?"

"I pushed all of us to take the job. And..." His lip curls.

I shake my head. "We all agreed to it. We thought the money was good. That there was no reason why we *shouldn't* have taken the money. We had to."

"I just wish I could have said good-bye," he says softly.

"I didn't get to say good-bye, either. It all happened so fast, and..." I squeeze my eyes shut. "We need to figure out what that was."

"How?"

I suppress a shudder at the very thought. "We call our employer. I'll put 45 million Space Yen on the fact that he knew what would happen."

"Hey now, you know I don't like losing. Besides, you should probably change first," PC says, a touch of amusement in his voice. "You don't want everyone to see you waterlogged. They may get mad that you wasted that much water."

And, despite everything, I smile.

THE ENTIRE CREW is on the bridge, even Oliver, who I feel like I should have helped a bit more to get over this. I make sure to walk out there with my head held high and my shoulders back. I need to put on a brave face for everyone. I need to let them know that we aren't dead in space.

I catch Orion's eyes as I head toward the captain's console and take a seat in Louis's old chair. I sweat; it still feels warm from him, even though my internal thermometer says that it's no warmer than the rest of the room.

Orion looks…calm. Much calmer than the rest of the crew, which I draw strength from. He may be an android, but there's something nice about having someone not freaked out like everyone else.

"Clem," Daisy says softly, but I pointedly ignore her before I lose my nerve. PC shakes his head at her as he takes his usual spot.

"Orion," I command, my voice wavering slightly. "Set up a com link to Chairman Maas of Syn-Tech. We have some questions we need to discuss. *Immediately.*"

The android blinks for a moment, processing my request, before keying in the call to the Chairman. I hope he picks up. It will be very telling if he doesn't—I know it will be because he knows exactly why I'm calling as opposed to being busy. If these patents in the /infinity folder are so important to him, he'd be sure to have his com always available in case we need help.

And I'm going to tear him a new one.

The call is accepted, and the Chairman's face fills the

screen. Where I once thought was perfectly coifed hair and flawless complexion, I now see the cracks and despise everything I see about him.

"Where is the captain?" he asks, his voice filling up the bridge in a more thunderous, commanding manner than I would have thought possible. He thinks he owns us, like he owns the Lifers for Syn-Tech. Except, in his eyes, we're expendable. He thinks we're expendable. Lower than low.

I purse my lips, trying to keep a lid on my fury. "He's now part of a table inside a hermetically sealed room, along with the rest of my arm." I lift up my stump for good measure. "I'm the acting captain of the ship. My name is Clementine Jones."

"Oh dear," Maas says, "I'm so sorry to hear that, Miss Jones. Will he be okay?" There's no emotion in his voice.

"Whatever you had me download on that ship—the *Nova*," I say, "there was some sort of weird virus, wasn't there? Something that I downlooted and it infected Captain Louis, and it infected whoever that was on the *Nova* with us."

Maas raises an eyebrow. "There was a creature on the *Nova* as well? We had thought they were destroyed when the Feds attacked the ship."

That explains the holes and the state that the ship was in when we found it. And that explains why it had been left drifting towards a blackhole. Why waste a perfectly good nuclear weapon when it was already headed towards being destroyed? They must have thought Syn-Tech would have been crazy for trying to recover it.

I guess they didn't count on Maas hiring space pirates.

"Why would the Feds have attacked that ship?" I ask, even though I can guess the answer. Maas even waits, letting me know that we're both in each other's orbit.

"The *Nova* was a research vessel," he says. "And it was there on that ship that they developed some of Syn-Tech's most, ah, *inspiring* intellectual properties."

Inspiring my ass. I clench my hand.

"What was that property?"

Maas's eyes narrow. "I believe you're intelligent enough to guess."

I have to swallow back my angry outburst. It's almost too hard to do so, but I maintain my composure. I can see that PC is about to explode.

"It was in the 'Infinity' folder?" I ask in an attempt to keep the conversation moving.

A half smile curves the Chairman's lips. "Correct. Contained within that is what's known as the Infinity Virus."

"And what's the Infinity Virus?"

Maas clasps his hands and steeples his fingers as he considers my question. "A lot of that is on a need-to-know basis, Miss Jones."

Of course. And I hate that he's calling me "Miss Jones" instead of "Captain." It's just another way he's trying to lord over me with his rank.

"I think," I say through gritted teeth, "that you sent my crew across the galaxy on a fool's errand—knowing that there was something dangerous on that ship—and you deemed us not worthy of making it out of there alive."

"Oh, that's where you're wrong," Maas says. He clicks his tongue in disappointment. "I'm so sorry to hear that you think so low of me. No, I hired the crew of the *Picara* because you were able to easily evade the *Nautilus's* security systems. SynTech knew that you had the highest chance of survival. And the Infinity Virus is so important to my company."

I rise to my feet. "At the expense of the crew?"

"You're not asking the right questions, Miss Jones." He pauses for emphasis. "What if I told you that there was a cure for this virus? That your beloved Captain Stevenson isn't beyond our help? Granted, possibly not in the same state as he was previously, but he doesn't have to be bound to a table for the rest of his life. We can retrieve his consciousness and find a host body."

I narrow my eyes, not believing the words that I'm hearing. "How?"

Maas grins wickedly in return. "We have been working on an antivirus for Infinity. It is incomplete as of yet, which is why we needed the virus from the *Nova*. Without it, we would have never been able to have finished the cure."

"Yeah, but with it, you need a cure," PC mutters under his breath.

I don't chide him for his outburst, not like Louis did. For however long it will be, I will be my own kind of captain for the *Picara*.

"So what must we do?"

"My offer still stands, despite your insubordination," Maas says. "300 million Space Yen for the return of the virus—*in person*. And we can cure your captain. And anyone else who may be infected."

Shit. That means that we still have to make our way to Alpha, which is clear across the Milky Way. And that's putting us right in Maas's clutches. And then the last part of his statement catches my attention.

"What do you mean, anyone else who may be infected?"

He chuckles deeply, and the sound reverberates all the way to my bones. "The Infinity Virus is unlike anything the universe has ever seen before." He sounds damn proud of it too, which sets my teeth on edge. "If you think that it's safe wherever you have it now, you're wrong. Once it figures out the makeup of the structures around it, it *will* find a way out. And whoever *downlooted* the initial file could possibly be infected. That wouldn't be your captain, by chance?"

Ice fills my veins at the weight of his words. *I* was the one who downlooted the virus. *I* was the one who brought it on this ship. I look over at the remains of my cyborg arm.

"Ah," Maas says, his voice satisfied, "apparently that was *you*. And there's a high chance now that you've infected everyone on the bridge along with you *and* everything on your ship. The only way to live beyond this run is to bring the virus to me."

I shiver.

In front of me, I see that PC mutes our coms. "He's bluffing," he says, but he doesn't sound like he believes himself. "He's bluffing because he wants the virus. And we have to be the ones to bring it to him."

"What if he's right?" Venice asks. He looks like he's just seen a space ghost. "I'm just a cook. I never wanted to be a part of this." His gaze turns on to me, and his mouth gapes in horror. "You're killing us."

Even Oliver's lip trembles, and I feel my stomach drop at the realization that the kid is frightened for his life now.

"No, she is not," Orion cuts in. He clasps his hands behind his back, standing straighter. "I have run a scan of Clementine during this conversation, and she is showing no signs of any infection."

"Yes, but Maas just said that this virus is nothing like anything we've ever seen," Venice mutters.

Orion glares at him, and the old man shrinks back. "I assure you, there is nothing about her physiology that would suggest her system has been compromised. Other than her missing arm, she is in good health."

Other than my arm that is stuck with what's left of Louis.

"Your crew seems to be on mute even as you're talking to each other," Maas says. He gives a smug chuckle. "Discussing whether you want to take the chance? I assure you, I am correct. If you don't come to Alpha, you might as well direct your ship into that blackhole, because you're going to die anyways. And infect the rest of the galaxy while you're at it."

"He's bluffing," PC hisses.

I hesitate before I turn on the mic again. "Give us some time to think. And...mourn," I say raggedly. "We have a lot to discuss."

"And not a lot of time in which to do it," Maas adds. "I give your ship seventy-three hours before you have an outbreak so bad, you can't contain it. And by that point, it'll be too late for my company to save you."

I turn my head slightly towards Orion. "We can make it to Alpha in just under fifty-six hours," he murmurs softly, looking down at the computer screen. On it is a route that he just mapped to Alpha.

Fifty-six hours. Cutting it too damn close. We can't wait around.

"I'll be in touch, Chairman," I say through gritted teeth, reaching to end the call.

"It's still 300 million Space Yen," Maas says, "and your lives and that of the universe."

I don't answer as I end it, and the screen goes black before showing the sea of stars beyond us.

Daisy spins around in her chair and speaks for the first time. "Screw the money," she says. Her teeth chatter and not from the cold. "I'm more concerned about staying alive at this point."

Chapter 14

Orion and PC are the only ones who dare to sit next to me in the mess hall. Everyone else is huddled at the end of the table, giving us as wide a berth as possible. We silently eat the bland food that Venice prepared. No one even comments on the taste. In fact, we all barely have a few bites before plates are pushed away. The cook doesn't even complain as he puts down his fork.

Earlier, Orion had done another medical scan of me, using the more sensitive equipment in the infirmary, and nothing came up. That didn't do much to assure the crew that I wasn't infected.

And I feel the same way. I don't feel like I'm fine. Furthermore, I don't feel safe, not with Louis the way he is and not with that room still sealed. I asked Orion to pull up the video feed for it again to see what's happening in there, but there's something obscuring the camera. Like something grew over it.

We have no idea what's happening in there. And I'm not about to let someone check it out.

And now, we have a decision to make.

"So," I say softly.

"So what?" Venice snarls.

PC opens his mouth to make a retort, but I shoot him a look.

"We need to figure out what we're doing next." I look around the table and see that everyone looks miserable and frightened for their lives—and with good reason, too. I can't imagine what must be going through their heads, if they're wondering if they'll live another week, another month. What's 300 million Space Yen when you're dead?

We also need to figure out how we're supposed to stay alive.

No one responds to me, not even Orion or PC. We're all lost in our thoughts, wondering what the fuck is happening to us. And I think the only person who knows for sure is Chairman Maas, and I don't trust him at all.

Then again, we can't afford to be foolish.

"I don't want to die," Daisy says.

"Neither do I," Oliver whimpers. His bottom lip trembles, and he watches the table, like he's too afraid to look at us. Protectively, Daisy wraps an arm around his shoulders, giving him an affectionate rub. I realize that I'm too afraid to touch him, in case I am infected.

I swallow nervously. "This is something that we need to discuss together."

"Because that worked *so* well last time," Venice mutters. Even Daisy shoots him a dirty look.

"That's something that we all have to own," I say. "We voted together. We made the decision together. This is what happened next. And now, we need to decide together if we're going to deliver this virus to Alpha. Or any other options."

"If we bring the virus to the Chairman," Taka muses, speaking up for the first time since I got out of the shower, "then he'll have the virus."

That was something I'd been considering as well. What would Syn-Tech do with something like the virus in their clutches? I don't want to be held responsible for delivering something so destructive to a company that may use it against others. I keep thinking about the arachni-lift and Louis…

But to do that, we'd have to put our lives at risk. *Again.*

"You know, I'd say no," Venice says, crossing his arms as he sits back. "In fact, I want to be let off this ship at the next port. Screw all y'all. I'm done."

"Fine," I say through gritted teeth. "You're relieved of your duties. But that may be after we make the drop."

The old man just glowers at me from his spot at the table.

"But if we don't go to Alpha," Daisy says, "then Louis is definitely gone."

"I know," I say with a nod. I comb a hand through my hair. "That's something that we'll have to take into consideration." I don't know if I can live with the knowledge that we didn't try *everything* to save Louis.

Then again, what can we do?

PC lets out an exasperated sigh through his nose. "As I said, I think Maas is bluffing."

"And he very well could be bluffing," I admit. "But…can we afford to take that chance?"

"And that's why you're terrible at poker," he quips. And the absurdity of his comment almost makes me smile. Almost.

"May I suggest," Orion says, "that we do fly closer to Alpha? Not go there necessarily, but we would be within flying distance in case any one of us starts showing symptoms. Or if we eventually do decide to deliver the virus. Being in the vicinity at least gives us that chance."

No one speaks as we all consider his words.

"That makes the most sense," Taka says.

"Yeah, but that also brings us closer to Syn-Tech," Daisy says. "What if he's counting on that?"

"I believe that between Taka and me, we can figure out how to mask the *Pícara* from radar," Orion offers, nodding towards the engineer. Taka blinks in surprise at being included. "We already have stealth technology. It is just a matter of making it more robust. That will at least keep Syn-Tech away for a time."

"Taka, do you think you can do that?" I ask gently.

He looks at me, wide eyed, before he nods.

"Okay, so that is an option," I say.

"Then I say aye," Daisy says.

Taka nods. "Yes."

I look at Venice. "I still say no," he mutters, averting his eyes.

Fine, I want to growl at him. "Oliver?"

The boy only nods.

PC lets out a sigh. "Then yes from me, too. Why the hell not?"

And that's already a majority in favor. Still, though, I glance at Orion. "It makes the most logical sense," he says.

I guess that's all I'll get from the android.

"All right," I say slowly. "Then we set course to put us in Alpha's vicinity. And we'll go from there."

Venice scoffs angrily. I choose to ignore him.

WE SET course for a part of space that is five lightdays from Alpha. It's as close as we dare to get to Alpha in such a busy part of space while being close enough should we decide to head to the spaceport. In case someone has the virus. In case I accidentally infected them.

The mood on the bridge is somber, pensive. And I'm not helping as I'm the one who commands the *Pícara* to fly there. It should be Louis doing this.

I can't help but feel like I'm shitting on Louis's memory by jumping in the role of acting captain so quickly.

Afterwards, it takes Taka and Orion over two hours to reach a solution that they're happy with. By that point, I'm the only person who's left on the bridge with them, as Daisy took Oliver to bed earlier in the night. PC went to bed as well, I think, to grieve Louis's death.

And Venice decided that he wanted nothing to do with us after our decision. Fine by me. I'll allow him that space. It's his right to feel however he wants.

It still doesn't seem right to sit in Louis's chair, so I'm in my own, lost in my own thoughts while the two of them work on the captain's console, having high-level access to everything on the *Pícara*.

I remember the goop coming out of Louis's spacesuit, the reds, yellows, and whites bleeding out on the table, leaking out, spreading towards me. Getting on my shoes, leeching up my body, until it gets into my mouth. There's a noise that I'm hearing. I think it's screaming. *I'm* the one who's screaming.

"Kill me," I hear Louis whisper, even over my own voice. *"I don't want to live like this. Kill me. Please kill me now."*

And it's too late for me to stop it...

"That's it!" Taka exclaims, and I jump out of my daydream. "That's it! That's it!"

I cough, trying to cover up my shock over his outburst. Orion doesn't miss it, though, and I see his smirk. Odd how an android can have so many different expressions.

"You guys got it figured out?" I ask, walking over to them.

"Oh, yes," Taka says, his fingers thrumming together. For a moment, I wonder if he's been infected like my cyborg hand had been. Then I remember that Taka gets like this when he's overly excited. "Yes, we have it definitely figured out. No one would be able to find us, not even if they knew where to look."

"How so?" I ask, leaning against the computer to get a peek of it.

"It is based on a principle of technology from old Earth,"

Orion says, his mouth pulled into a smile. "We have reprogrammed the *Picara's* shields to take on a shape that reflects radar signals away from us. On radar, we will look like the rest of the galaxy."

"You can just do that with the shields?" I ask in disbelief.

Orion nods. "It required some creative thinking, but it should be fully functional."

I still don't quite follow them. "Why hasn't it been tried before? How do you know it will work?"

"Trust us, Clem," Taka says, giving me a proud pat on the shoulder as he passes by me. "We're safe. Now it's time for me to go to bed." And just like that he waltzes out of the bridge, dancing with an imaginary partner, humming something to himself. The man is on space cloud nine, and I can't help but smile after him.

He's a strange one, definitely.

"He is brilliant," Orion says, and I glance back at him. Did I say that out loud? "Taka is able to take the best parts of machines and wires and apply a different kind of logic to it. It was his idea to reshape the shields."

I sigh, putting my hand on my hip. "And imagine, he's a space pirate with that genius."

"I do trust that he is happy. To humans, that seems to matter the most."

I reflect on his words for a moment. "How do you do that?"

"Do what?"

"Dissect what we're feeling into only a few words. You make me feel like I'm transparent."

"I am an android. It is my duty to analyze the human condition and improve upon it." He closes a few screens on the panel and shuts down the console, setting the *Picara* on autopilot. Fifty-three hours and we'll be so close to Alpha, we can spit on it. And we'll be that much closer to civilization if this turns out to be bad.

Louis's liquid form flashes in my mind, and I shudder.

"How are you finding tasks with just one arm?"

"Hmm?" I ask, blinking at him.

"Your arm." He nods over to me. "You have been missing it since just after you came back on the ship."

I look down at my right stump, at the wires dangling from it. It feels like that hand is completely alien to me now, a separate piece from me. I had been so wholly dependent on that arm before, using it to downloot other ships' data, as my dominant hand—everything.

Funny how it hasn't been too big of a deal now.

"I suppose I should find my old hand," I say distractedly. Louis had suggested the same thing when he was trying to fix it.

"You have an old part?"

I flinch at Orion's use of the word "part," but I suppose that's what it is. I'm over half cyborg. I have parts that can be repaired, fixed, and changed. It feels odd after what happened to Louis.

"Yeah, I think it's in a supply closet somewhere around here."

Honestly, I have no idea where it is, since it's been nearly ten years since I needed it, and I purged that information from my memory banks a long time ago. I know I have it, though. Cyborg parts are so expensive, those who opt to upgrade their bodies have to make the difficult decision as to whether or not they want to sell the old parts secondhand or keep it in case of a malfunction. I was lucky enough to decide on the latter. As a space pirate, you can never be too careful with your body parts. You never know when you'll be shot.

So we both dig through all of the extra storage rooms and turn my bedroom upside down before we spot it in the kitchen pantry, up on the highest shelf behind some canned goods. "How the hell did it get up here?" I ask, standing on my tiptoes on a stepladder.

"It must be from the many times the *Pícara* was stocked," Orion says, nodding towards the hand. "Things get shifted when that happens."

"Yeah. At least it's here." I blow the dust off it, making me cough. Ten years have passed by since I needed it. And that was back before life got complicated.

"It's a lot smaller than I remember," I muse as I step down from the ladder. "But I've got it." My retina tells me that it's fifteen percent smaller than my newer one—which is in quarantine with the mutated table—but the difference might as well be huge. You know your body better than anyone, so a slight change could really set you off-kilter.

"You still have the nails painted," Orion adds, and I give a little laugh, noticing the pink on the ends of my fingertips.

"I took really good care of this, didn't I? Well, here's hoping that pink matches my new style." I know that it doesn't, but I'm too tired to really care.

"I assume you need help reattaching it?" Orion asks. "Your left hand is less dexterous than your right, correct?"

I lick my lips. "Yeah, but…" The last person to try to repair my arm is now as good as dead. And if Maas *is* correct and I have something sinister in me, then I don't want anyone trying again. I keep thinking about that finger cutting through tough spacesuit fabric.

"Clementine," Orion says, his voice steadying me, "I don't sense the virus in you. It is fine."

I nod. "You're right." Although I really don't want to put him at any risk, android or no.

I bump into a jar of clear liquid. It's a stash of Venice's moonshine. Even just looking at it makes me want to gag as I remember it burning all the way down my throat. I'm about to brush it off but then think better of it.

What's a better excuse to get drunk than having your father-figure die while detaching your arm? I tuck my replacement part underneath my right armpit and grab the jar.

"What are you doing?" Orion asks.

"Numbing myself."

He frowns after me. "But any sensation you will feel is an electrical impulse to simulate pain. I can turn it off if you need a numbing agent."

"It's not my arm that needs to be numb." I sit down at the table and wedge the jar between my knees to unscrew the lid. I chug a good mouthful of it, and it sears my throat and settles somewhere in my chest, where it roasts. The taste is just as awful as ever.

And that makes it all right.

Orion gives me one more look, and then he sits down and opens up a storage compartment in his forearm, featuring a set of repair tools. "All right, let us get started."

Chapter 15

I drink—a *lot*—while Orion reattaches my arm. It does a lot to help dull my senses. But it doesn't do enough to take my mind off everything.

"D'you think that Maas was telling the truth?" I slur, leaning into Orion. "That he has a cure for the virus?"

Orion keeps working, even through my questions, his attention always in multiple places at once. "That is up for debate."

"I know." I take a swig. "But I wanna know what you think."

"What I *think* is entirely different than facts."

"Just answer the question, Orion." I sigh. Sometimes, talking to an android is like talking to a wall. They can be just like people in the best times and just like a tool in the most inopportune times. What I need right now is a friend and not a robot.

"I believe that there is the possibility of it," he says finally. "Syn-Tech is a pharmaceutical company that manufactures vaccines and medication for the entire galaxy. There has been some speculation in the past that they have treated most every ailment known to biological organisms that they have started manufacturing their own." He glances up at me. "But that is pure conjecture."

"You mean like the Space Flu?" The Space Flu was a devastating disease that devastated millions of people on the planet Kazo-Pharmacology about thirty years ago. I remember reading about it in the newsfeeds—it just came out of nowhere and nearly killed the whole population of Kazo's Lifers and damaged their reputation, as no one wanted to trade with a company that could potentially make them sick. A disease that we have no immunity to is far scarier than even space battles.

I remember reading some conspiracy theories that it had been coordinated by a rival company. No evidence, other than it left a crippled company in its wake.

He shrugs. "As I said, pure conjecture."

I somber, watching him work on my arm. "Is it bad that I hope there is a cure?" I murmur. "I don't want us to be sick, and I don't care about the money, but I want Louis to be all right. He deserves better than what he got. And if I can help him…"

"We shall assess Captain Louis's odds closer to Spaceport Alpha," Orion assures me. "Everything about this is taking into account the risks and benefits. And I am not one of those androids who does not value human life."

I smile sadly. "So you think he's worth saving? Even with the known risks?"

"I believe in taking a certain amount of precaution. But no matter how we look at it, there is still a highly dangerous lifeform on the *Pícara* that we may not be able to contain for much longer."

"And if the rest of us are infected, too?"

He stops suddenly. "This is done. Try moving your hand."

I look down at my arm for the first time in what feels like ages. The arm is fully attached now. The splice where the arm meets the rest of my upper arm and shoulder isn't pretty, and I have a large ridge where it's too skinny, but...

I wriggle my fingers, and they respond exactly how I want them to. My retina tells me that due to the smaller size of the hand, my electrical signals are sent microseconds faster, so I should allot less time for my actions.

"It works," I say, holding up my hand for him to see. "Thank you, Orion."

He gives a curt nod, his eyes brilliant in the fluorescent light of the mess hall. I've noticed them before, but for some reason, I can't take my eyes off them now.

"It is my duty," he says, looking at his own hand. The tools that peek out of his hand fold away into a working, humanoid hand. "And while it isn't a permanent solution, it should suffice for now."

"For now," I agree, taking another mouthful of moonshine. And I look at the empty jar confusedly as I set it down. Wasn't it full when I started drinking?

"Your blood alcohol content is at 0.13%," Orion says, standing. I'd ignored the warning in my retina, but the fact that he notices as well makes me frown. "Your motor functions and judgment are impaired as a result." He extends a hand towards me.

"Oh. I don't feel that way."

There's another one of those devastating smiles. "Then your goal to become 'numb' must have worked."

I chuckle lightly as he pulls me to my feet. Like earlier, I'm unsteady, but instead of it being caused by grief and fear, this is just from me being drunk. Just the way I wanted to be. I look up at him, noticing the height difference between us. He seems so tall sometimes. So human. I look at his perfect features and wonder who his maker sculpted him after. Full lips. Kissable lips.

And I wonder why I haven't tasted them yet...

I close my eyes, lean forward, and put my mouth on his.

His lips are softer than I would have thought for being a robot, no different than any other man's lips I've kissed. They're warm too, and even though he doesn't respond to my kiss, I lean into it, trying to coax him to kiss me back.

For a moment, he's rigid underneath my fingertips, and I know that I've caught him off-guard. Hell, I'm off-guard as well. And drunk. So very drunk.

"What are you doing?" he asks, pulling back from me.

Shit. Shit. Shit.

I take in a shuddering breath, feeling the heat come to my cheeks. My retina tells me that my heartrate is increased and my internal temperature is up. I'm fucking embarrassed now. "Uhm…" I don't have an answer for his question. Just this shame that burns through me.

"Clementine." The way he says my name makes me flinch. No longer is he the gentle android that helped repair my arm. He's back into full-robot mode, and looking at him, I don't know how I could have ever thought he looked human. There's a coldness to him, a severity that marks him as something *other*.

"I'm sorry," I say as I turn away, wiping off the sensation of his lips against mine with the back of my hand. "I didn't mean to—" I make to move away from him and to get back to my quarters where I want to fall asleep and drink off my stupor. And hopefully believe myself that I was just drunk when I kissed him.

My feet tangle up in themselves, and I stumble, falling forward. Orion's strong arms wrap around me, grasping me by the upper arms.

"You are not fit to walk by yourself," Orion says, but I shrug him off. Luckily, this time I don't fall.

"I'm fit 'nough to be mortified," I say, stalking out of the mess hall. My anger and embarrassment are enough focus to help me walk upright as I head towards my quarters. Now, which way was it? There are a few ways to get my room, but I can't remember which is the shortest.

Why does everything seem fuzzy to me right now?

Well, you wanted to be numb. Thanks for the moonshine, Venice.

"Clementine!" Orion calls behind me. Like a robot, there's no desperation to his voice, which is another item on the list to reinforce why I shouldn't have kissed him.

I ignore him and finally make my decision, taking a left on the way to my room. It's the shorter way to my quarters, and unlike the time when Orion walked me back after poker, there's no nice conversation between us.

He calls my name once again, but I ignore him as I palm the lock screen on my door to open. I get an immediate rejection, and it takes me a moment to realize what went wrong.

Wrong hand, dumbass. The touchpad was keyed to my other cyborg hand.

I key in the manual code, and the door hisses open. And not a moment too soon.

"Clementine, please talk to me!" Orion says, too close for me to risk looking back at him, and I step inside my room and palm the screen to close the door behind me, effectively sealing him outside. He can very easily key in the code to enter himself, or call me, but as seconds stretch into moments, I realize that he won't.

My heart pounds in my chest, and I debate whether or not I should head to the restroom and puke up my guts or if I should lay down and see if I can sleep off the alcohol.

In the end, exhaustion wins, and I nearly collapse on my too-hard mattress. I pull up my thin blanket and roll on my side, drawing my legs up to my chest. I look at my right hand and slowly bend each knuckle, one at a time, until I make a fist.

In the morning, I'll explain away the kiss as a moment of insanity brought on by the combination of grief and alcohol.

No one would fault me for wanting to have a sense of being wanted after brushing death so many times.

Right?

As I try to sleep, I can't help this hollow, empty feeling inside that doesn't have to do with any of it.

And I wonder, not for the first time, if I truly can call myself human.

Chapter 16

"Ugh, fuck," I mutter, combing my right hand through my hair. The dim fluorescent light in my quarters is still too bright. I drank way too much last night. Louis is going to be pissed at me.

I freeze at the thought of Louis. Everything comes back to me all at once, what happened to him, where we're headed now. Tears spring into my left eye, but I fight them off. I look, almost in horror, at my old cyborg hand, how much smaller it is than what I'm used to.

It's all real. Every bit of it.

Suddenly, there's not enough air for me to properly breathe, and my retina is telling me, once again, that I'm hyperventilating. The hangover blossoms to a crippling headache behind my eye sockets. I rub my eyes, and I grimace at the memory of *everything*.

And the cherry on top of all the shit that happened? I kissed Orion.

Everything is so fucked up. All I want to do is crawl under my blanket and fall back asleep and hide from the galaxy and the world.

Take a shower first. Then go on from there.

I stumble to my en suite and turn on the water to the shower. The spray comes out boiling hot and too fast, burning my hand as I snatch it out of the way.

"Ugh, fuck off, *Pícara!*" I yell to the ship, grimacing. "Just let me take a damn shower!"

It's just another insult to add to my injured peace of mind from yesterday. The water still comes out hot, steaming, but it goes down to a trickle, as if the ship is simmering mad at me. She was kind enough to me yesterday to let me sit in the shower for as long as I wanted, but this may be her way of trying to snap me out of it. Or showing me that she'll never treat me as well as Louis.

Louis…

I press my head to the steel of the wall next to the shower. "I'm sorry." I close my eyes. "I miss him, too. I'm…*trying*…to figure out how to bring him back. I promise."

A second later, the water temperature goes back to warm at the appropriate pressure level. I give a nod. "Thank you."

I shower within the ration time, and even in that three minutes, I feel more rejuvenated than when I first woke up. Still not great, but at least I'm steady on my feet. I towel dry my hair and put on a fresh uniform, forgoing my makeup, as it feels like it's too much.

I step out of my quarters, feeling marginally more human than I did when I first woke up.

I head to the bridge and pause in the doorway as I see Orion standing with his hands clasped behind his back. His gaze is on the window, watching the streaks of stars as they shoot by. He turns his head towards me, his face impassive.

Of course it would be. Did I expect him to apologize? Or say that he wanted to kiss me more?

I force back the lump in my throat. "Good morning." He only gives an affirmative nod in my direction.

Fine then, we'll just act like this is all strictly business. *I can do this.*

I stride stiffly towards Louis's captain's chair—*my* chair now—and take a seat. "Where are we currently?"

Orion's mouth curves up to a distant smile as he turns back to the window. "Currently forty-six hours from our destination," he says.

A little over two days. I drum the fingers of my right hand on the armrest. "Not much we can do then," I say.

"It appears so," Orion says.

Just nearly two days of nothing to do other than have these awkward conversations between us. I need PC here. Or Daisy or Taka. Or even Oliver, as he would be a distraction. I check some diagnostics of the ship, making sure that everything is well stocked. I even check the cameras for the quarantine room. They're still covered up, which is worrisome.

What the hell am I supposed to do with that?

"Listen, Clementine—" Orion says, his voice sounding unusually strained.

Flutters in my stomach. I don't want to hear what he has to say, to dig the knife in a little further. I'm already embarrassed enough as it is. I crossed a line last night, and I have to deal with it.

Apparently not now.

I get back to my feet, unable to sit down. "I'm going to see what Venice cooked in the mess hall," I say. "So carry on."

The android watches me as I walk back to the door. He opens his mouth to say something but then closes it and only nods.

I step through the door, and it shuts behind me with a forceful *snap*. The ship was mad at me first, and now she's acting belligerent because I'm avoiding Orion? She can't have it both ways.

I roll my eyes. "Now's not the time for that," I mutter. "One thing at a time."

For forty-six hours, I'll take everything one by one.

And figure out what to do from there.

THE TRIP to our little patch of empty space is uneventful. I can tell that the crew is ill at ease with all that has been happening, so the downtime is welcome, even if we're avoiding the elephant-class ship in the room. We don't speak all that often to each other, our meals in the mess hall are quiet, and no one goes near the part of the ship with the quarantine room.

We're trying to pretend that everything is all right and failing horribly at it.

I hate sitting in Louis's chair, at how it feels like it was meant for a larger man with more experience.

I split my time between the bridge and quarters, curled up on the bed and wishing for a different outcome. My retina tells me that I need to take some serotonin to get my hormone levels back to where they should be.

After what's happened, I think I should allow myself to be depressed and traumatized.

My general state of mind seems to be all that's wrong with me, though. I don't show any other symptoms of the virus, even though I constantly ask Orion to scan me. It's not popping up anywhere in my body. I don't know whether to believe him or to still think that it's in my body, waiting to come out and turn me into goop. Or worse, turn the crew into goop.

It doesn't help that I can't get rid of the memory of the kiss with Orion. Long after my headache faded, I have a different sort of headache in tiptoeing around the subject with him. He doesn't bring it up, but I catch him looking at me from time to time. Probably wondering why a cyborg thought it was all right to kiss a navigator android.

I wish I could just laugh it off and say that I confused him for a pleasure android when I was drunk. But that seems like it's too far-fetched. I may have been inebriated, but I knew exactly what I was doing when I kissed him.

So forty-six hours passes by, full of tension and unspoken words.

A great way to start my time as captain.

I FEEL the G-forces on my body increase drastically and then release me as the ship comes out of FTL. I take a deep breath, filling my shrunken lungs with oxygen as I straighten up, giving a loud cough. The restraints have cut into my body, leaving bruises where I have flesh.

"I hate coming out of FTL," PC mutters, echoing my sentiment. He clears his throat and rolls his shoulders.

The view from the bridge shows tightly packed stars a few lightyears from our position. We're alone in this space, but I didn't realize how disconcerting it would be to know that Syn-Tech Alpha is only a few lightdays away.

I feel exposed here, like they're a neighboring ship that can look through our windows and see us naked. And I hate it.

"Are the shields holding?" I ask, glancing at Taka. I hope I don't sound as frightened as I feel.

The engineer nods as he looks at his screen. "Everything is holding. Radar is pinging off us, and we're effectively invisible to everyone."

"Unless they look right at us," PC says, crossing his arms.

Taka levels him with his gaze. "The odds of that are slim to none. Do you know how vast space is?"

"Do you know how many things have lined up to fuck us

over?" PC quips. I flinch at his words, and my surrogate brother gives me a reproachful look.

So we just wait here for a while. And see if we're infected. If we're not, then we just figure out what to do with the quarantine room—or if I decide to try to save Louis, which I'm still grappling with. And if we're infected...then we're close enough to put our lives in Syn-Tech's hands.

"You couldn't have dropped me off at a spaceport or anything?" Venice mutters with a sneer, lost in his own thoughts.

"No," I shoot back. "No, we couldn't."

"We have plenty of time to take me to another company's port. Vanheim Gamma or something."

"We can't," I say.

The cook glares at me. "Can't or don't want to?"

"Venice," Daisy growls. "*Stop.*"

Venice opens his mouth to make a retort, but the big woman cocks her head, a warning in her gaze, and he finally throws up his arms and rises from his seat. "You're going to kill all of us," he says, pointing a finger at me. "You're going to kill all of us because you're refusing to do the right thing and *get me out of here.*"

"We're a crew," I tell him. "We make decisions together. And we can't let you go, not until we know that we're not infected."

"Well, I want out," he says. "You were the one who brought the virus here. And you're going to kill us all."

He storms out of the bridge, leaving me glaring at a spot on my console because I'm afraid to look up and see the expressions of the rest of the crew. Do they feel the same way he does? I don't want them to feel like I'm killing them by keeping them here.

But surely they know that we can't leave and expose the virus to anyone else?

"Hey, Clem," PC says.

"I'm fine," I say through gritted teeth. "I think his food will taste particularly angry tonight."

"I'd be lying if I said I wasn't scared," Daisy says, "but we can't let him go. Not until we know for sure."

Taka nods in agreement.

At least I can reason with most of the crew. I glance over at Orion, who is watching our exchange with a sense of detachment. I wish I could take away my emotions like he does.

"Orion," I command, tightening my ponytail, "maintain our position for the next three days. And if you see anything suspicious—ships coming back, weird space activity, *anything*—then we need to move."

"Yes, captain," he says stoically.

Like he's been ever since I kissed him.

It's all so messed up. I wish Venice wasn't mad at me, or else I'd raid the pantry again and grab another jar of moonshine. But I don't think he'd go for that at all at the moment.

"So," Taka says, "what do we do now?"

"Well, I'm going to relax for a bit," I announce.

Taka exchanges a glance with Daisy. "I mean, what do we do while we're here?" he says.

"We just wait," I say. And I don't add if we're waiting to see if we're infected or to die or…

I can't stand it anymore. I offer a small smile. "We'll figure it out."

I hate lying.

I flee from the bridge and the crew that is depending on me to make the right decision. Truth is, I have no idea what to do from here. I do agree with Venice that we're waiting for our deaths. But the galaxy cannot afford for us to be wrong.

It can't afford for us to infect any others.

I wander the halls of the *Pícara*, running my left hand along the walls. I've been on this ship since I was little, and I remember doing the exact same thing when I was little, only much shorter. Finding a permanent home was a boon for PC and me, and the ship, apart from having its feud with me, has been a part of my life as long as Louis has.

So many memories in these halls. And it teeters at the moment on the edge of the unknown. I hate having unknowns. I'm sure it's driving Orion crazy to not be able to extrapolate different outcomes and make a recommendation.

It feels risky any way we slice it.

And the crew is depending on me.

I hear a sniffle above me, up in the crawl space. I remember being a child and hiding up there to get away from Louis when I was in trouble or when I wanted to get away from everyone. As such, I know exactly how to find him and get up there, and I crawl my way towards the youngest member of the crew.

Oliver is sitting in the dark, illuminated by the glow of his mini-tab as he reads on it. I see tears glistening in the poor light, and his face looks too drawn, too scared to be okay.

"Hey," I hail him softly.

He jumps at my voice and looks up. "Oh," he says. "Clementine. Er, Captain."

I smile despite myself. "It's still just Clementine," I say. "Clem, if you want to keep it short."

He looks confused for a moment. "Oh, I thought—"

I shake my head. "Don't worry about it. Just consider me a friend."

He nods slowly, distractedly.

"You okay?" I ask.

He hesitates. "No." His voice comes out as whimper.

I should have expected that answer. And the thing is, I'm not sure what to tell him. I don't want to tell him a lie, but I don't want him to spend however long terrified out of his mind. How do you stop a kid from seeing monsters every time he closes his eyes?

"We're trying to figure out what to do," I say. "But we will do everything we can to make sure we're all okay."

"Including Captain Louis?"

A lump forms in my throat. "We're trying to save him, too."

He nods again, not meeting my eyes. "I had bad nightmares last night."

I shift to sit closer to him. "What kind of nightmares?"

He chews on his bottom lip. "That I get sick. And I don't get well, and there's no way of fixing me. And you abandon me in space."

"Oh, Oliver," I say, wrapping an arm around his shoulders, and I feel the boy's sobs shake his small frame. "We won't let that happen. I will let myself get sick before I ever let anything happen to you."

He looks up at me, his eyes wide. "But what if we all get sick, Clementine? What if we can't fix this?"

"That's why we are where we are," I say. "We're close enough to people who say they can help us."

"So why aren't we there already?"

I've been grappling with that for a while now, and I don't have a good answer, other than I don't trust Maas to have our best interests at heart. Why would I after everything that's happened?

So I just sigh. "We're trying to make sure that we have the best information to make the best decision," I say gently. "We want to make sure that we don't make a mistake."

He's silent for a moment, thinking on my words. "I'm scared," he says softly. "I'm just really scared."

Now's when I'm completely honest with him. "I am, too. And it's okay to be scared. It just makes you alert and aware of everything that's happening. You'll be prepared."

"I don't feel that way." He flips through a page on his mini-tab, and there's a picture of a large reptile that supposedly lived on old Earth millions of years ago. And supposedly, they were wiped out too. I wonder if something like this virus got ahold of them and ripped through their species.

But I push that thought from my mind. "Between Daisy and me," I say, "we'll protect you, okay?"

He nods. "Thank you," he says.

I hope he feels some sort of relief. Because I'm still trying to figure it out myself.

Chapter 17

"These damn cameras," I mutter, flipping through the different views into the quarantine room.

"Still can't see?" PC asks, leaning in towards me to peer over my shoulder.

"Well, have a look," I say, indicating my screens.

Like the past few days, we see a filmy skin that only lets about ten percent of the light in and it obscures the rest of the view. They've been covered up with whatever's going on in that room, and I shudder to think what that is, if it's Louis or something else.

"That's…disturbing," he mutters under his breath. "What do you think is happening in there?"

I shake my head. "I don't know."

Is Louis's consciousness still in there? Is he wondering if we abandoned him? I hate that thought.

"What do you want to do?" PC asks under his breath.

"About Louis?"

"Yeah. It's been thirty-six hours since we arrived here."

I suck in a deep breath. We're outside of the incubation period that Maas had given us, that the ship would be so infested with the virus that we'd be begging for help. So far so good. I haven't shown any symptoms, and neither has anyone else, much to Venice's chagrin, who takes every moment to criticize our methods. He accuses me of keeping him against his will.

What he doesn't seem to understand is that all of this is against our will.

"I don't know," I sigh. "I'd hoped that there would have been...*something* different. But...it's all the same, isn't it?" I chew on the fingernails of my left hand. "What do we do if nothing changes?"

"Then we keep talking and keep evaluating," PC says.

"Well, it's hard to do that when I can't see what's happening." I shake my head and curse under my breath. "Why couldn't the *Pícara* have had windows down there?"

"Because then that would have been too easy." PC snickers softly, putting his hands on his hips. "But there's nothing we can do about it now."

"If everything's all right, should I go in there with a flamethrower?" I ask. "How will we get it off the ship?"

"If all that's true, then we can see about removing the room. And dropping it into a blackhole."

And that would cut into my budget for repairing the hole in my leg, which I'm still dealing with on top of everything else.

"Perfect," I say sarcastically.

PC smiles at me. "We'll figure it out, Clem. You always were bad at playing the long game."

"Well, I'm not going to figure anything out by looking at this." I turn off the screens with a snort of disgust. "I just wish something would go right."

He shrugs. "Things can only go so wrong before they eventually go right, right?"

I quirk an eyebrow at that.

"Speaking of things going awry," PC says, putting his

hands in his trouser pockets, "what's going on between you and Orion?"

Immediately, my internal systems send me a warning that I need to calm myself down, and a coolant kicks in to lessen the heat in my cheeks. "Nothing."

PC doesn't look convinced. "I know you, Clem. And you're a terrible liar. He's been acting weird for a few days now. Not talking to anyone."

I open my mouth but snap it shut and shake my head with a self-deprecating laugh. "I got drunk the night that Louis…" My voice trails off. "Orion reattached my old arm, and…I mistook him for a human."

"Mistook him how?"

I scratch my ear. "I kissed him."

PC's reaction is immediate. "That's a problem?"

"He's a navigator android, not a pleasure bot."

He shrugs. "Well, maybe the problem is that he liked it, too."

"He's an android, PC. He doesn't *like* things."

A lopsided smile comes to PC's face. "Don't sell yourself short, Clem. Did *you* like it?"

I don't want to tell him that I did. "I don't like where this conversation is going," I say, spinning in my chair as I stand. "I'm going to bed."

"Just remember, Clem," PC calls after me, "you're more machine than human. If you enjoyed it, maybe he did, too."

I give him a vulgar gesture before I leave him and head back to my quarters. Of course, out of everyone on the ship I can bump into, I run smack dab into Orion as I round a corner. As in, I'm so lost in my thoughts, I bounce off his hard chest.

"Careful, Captain," Orion says with that same distance he's had since I threw myself at him.

"Sorry," I mutter, averting my eyes. "I'm just trying to get to bed."

He nods. "That would be wise."

"Yeah." Then nervous laughter bubbles out of me. "Amazing how small the ship can seem, right?"

I make to move away from him, but he seems to be in my way. His eyes are watching me intently, and I try everything I can to not look up into them. To not lose myself in them.

"How are you?" he asks finally.

I snicker. "Well, I've been far better. I'd have to say that the past week has been the worst of my life. And nothing seems to be going right. But, sure. I'm fine. Peachy keen."

He only watches me.

"Well, have a good night," I say, pushing past him.

"Clementine," he says, using my name, which causes me to look back at him. I can't stand how good-looking he is, especially with everything that's happened. Yet another instance in which I screwed up.

Finally, he tilts his head in my direction. "Sweet dreams."

I'm about to turn away when a question comes to me. "Do androids have dreams?"

"If you mean that, when I power down, I have visions of possibilities, then, yes." He nods solemnly. "Yes, we do have dreams."

I raise both eyebrows in surprise. "That's…interesting."

"There are a lot about androids that would surprise you," he says.

I wonder if there's more to that, but I decide not to take him up on it. "Night," I say.

And then I flee to the safety of my room before I make even more of an ass out of myself. Thankfully, I fall asleep quickly.

But this time, I dream.

LIKE BEFORE, I walk with my fingertips brushing along the walls of the hallway. The *Picara* is dark though, far darker than it should be, like I'm standing in it while only the auxiliary power is on. My cyborg leg is whole once again, so my gait is even and full.

Lights flicker ominously, with only one out of four hallway lights actually working. I hear the drip of something echoing around me, like water or something else.

Then I hear the footsteps, a bunch of legs working in succession with each other, with something dragging behind it, like a broken limb. The arachni-lift. It's somewhere behind me, advancing ever so quickly.

I look behind me, feeling terror grip my heart, waiting for the abomination to show up. I don't know why I'm waiting, except I'm rooted to my spot, unable to continue.

Then the arachni-lift crashes into the corridor. The lone bloodshot eye sees me, and the human mouth opens and screeches like a predator finding its prey. The spell that it has on me is released, and I turn on my heel and run.

The *Picara* of my dreams is far bigger than in real life, with hallways that continually get narrower and narrower, pressing in on me as I flee. The space between the walls keeps getting smaller and smaller until I'm turned sideways and shuffling ever so slowly forward.

That doesn't seem to stop the arachni-lift behind me, though. I can hear it, getting ever so closer to me.

I cry out and stumble forward as the hallways suddenly open up, and I spill out in front of the quarantine room. The sounds of the arachni-lift behind me halt, and it doesn't follow me out into this space.

Relief spreads through me, and I feel safe for just a moment.

Then I turn to look at the room. I still can't see inside it, but I don't have to in order to know that there's something even worse than the arachni-lift brewing in there. Something sinister reaches out towards me, threatening to choke me.

It's nauseating, causing my stomach to flip, and I gag uncomfortably.

But something compels me to move forward. To finally figure out what's happening beyond the door.

I tentatively reach out and put my palm flat against the door.

An electric shock hits me, and I gasp.

But that's not the loudest sound I hear now. Ricocheting off the inside of my skull, there's a sound that I hear in my brain and not through my ears.

HELPME. HELPME. HELPME.

The ship. It's screaming at me, wanting me to help it. And it builds in crescendo until all I can do is scream along with it.

Whatever is happening inside that room, it's destroying the *Pícara*.

And I know that if I don't stop it, it's going to destroy us as well.

I WAKE up in a sweaty tangle of sheets and blankets, but I'm back in my room, by myself. The dim lighting in my room is exactly as it should be, and I don't hear the clanging of the arachni-lift following me.

I groan as I comb my small child's hand through my hair, trying to calm my racing heart.

"Fuck," I mutter. "Fucking hell."

Why is it that I don't dream when I want to, but when I finally do, it's a horrible nightmare about the very ship I'm on?

At least it wasn't real. I can tell myself that.

It's 0430, too early to get ready for the day, but I doubt I'll fall asleep again. Not after that dream.

A groan rips through the room, like metal expanding and compressing. I freeze and look up at the ceiling, wondering if that was the *Pícara* trying to talk to me or if we hit a particularly cold spot in space and I'm imagining it.

Another groan sounds, and I get to my feet in a start.

It is the ship. And she's trying to tell me something.

I shake my head, looking around, begging it to not be true. No, I don't want to see the quarantine room. I don't want to leave the safety of my room. And I don't want to face what could be happening.

I don't want the responsibility.

The light flickers again, oddly reminiscent of my dream, and I snarl as I slip my feet into my shoes. "I'm going, I'm going, I'm going," I mutter.

I palm open the door and pad silently toward the quarantine room. No one else is up yet, which is probably a good thing, but I feel like I'm dealing with ghosts now. There's an eeriness to everything, and dread clenches my stomach as I make my way there.

The *Pícara* makes no further indication that she's trying to tell me something, so I take that as her approval. For better or worse.

No arachni-lift, no narrowing corridors. So far, so good.

Then the quarantine room comes into view, and when I see it, I stop, trying to make sense of what I'm looking at. Because it doesn't make sense. Hell, even from my dream, what I'm seeing before me doesn't match anything in my memory bank.

What the...fuck?

The door to the quarantine room is overgrown with cobwebs of flesh. All around the doorframe, which is supposed to be airtight, there are chunks of flesh that flow outward, pulsating with….*something*. And beyond that, I can see the metal walls of the *Pícara* are pulsating too.

It's infected. Like Louis. Like my hand.

"Louis?" I whisper, wondering if that sack of flesh could still understand me. If there's still a piece of Louis in there.

There's movement in the corner of my eye. I lurch forward, meaning to get a better look at the captain.

And then I see Venice standing there.

"What the fuck are you doing here?" I blurt, staring agape at him.

He glowers at me. "I'm allowed to go anywhere in the ship." He sounds defensive, like I've caught him with his hand in the cookie jar.

"Yes," I say. "But why are you *here*?"

"Bad dream." He points at the door to emphasize his point. "There's something really, really wrong happening in there."

We can both see that. I look back at the door and feel revulsion shimmer down me, all the way to my circuits in my right toes. This is something far beyond my own ability to figure out or solve. This is a virus that's meaning to kill all of us.

It's going to infect the ship around us and then corner us until we give in.

I make the decision. I know what we have to do. If there's even the slightest chance we can stop this, then it's worth it. If we do nothing, we're going to die.

"We have to go to Alpha," I say through clenched teeth. "This is getting out of control. It's not getting better."

Venice whips his head towards me, snarling. "Don't you fucking dare! Do you know what'll happen there? They'll dissect us and use us for experiments!"

That may be true, but…what choice do I have?

"I'm sorry, Venice." I shake my head apologetically as I

close the distance between us. "We have to figure out how to get rid of this. And we may be infected even now."

"I'm not infected," he says, shaking his head. He gestures wildly at the thing that used to be our captain. "I'm not *that*!"

That's when I see the handheld zapper that he raises to fire at the combined mass of flesh and metal. My mind reacts faster than my body can, and I'm only able to get out one word before all hell breaks loose. "Don't—"

Venice fires, blasts of energy burning the creature. A loud, earsplitting shriek rips through the ship, inhuman and wordless, and we both wince in pain. Venice drops the zapper to cover his ears, even though that will do little to protect his eardrums. My bones rattle with the creature shrieking in pain.

With my own hands over my ears, I watch in horror as the creature lurches forward, whipping a swath of flesh towards him. It catches him across the face and spins him in a full circle before he collapses on the floor.

And that's not all…

"Help me," he gasps, grappling his ways towards me. I'm frozen to my spot as I watch him melt from the outside in. His cheeks first, then the top of his head, exposing his gray matter before that, too, turns to goo and spills out on the floor.

I stagger back a step but not before his hand strikes out and grabs me around the left ankle. My human ankle. His touch sears through me, and I seize up in pain as it rips through me as well. We're both infected and spreading the virus right now.

We couldn't stop the Infinity Virus. We're helping it spread.

My feet tangle up with each other as his grip is tight, and I hit the floor, hard, landing in a splash of *Venice*. Then I feel his hand dissolve as well and spill out around me.

Venice melted within minutes. How long do I have? How do I stop it from ravaging across my body?

"*Clementine?*" I hear a voice gasp. "What happened?"

I painfully wrench my head up to see Orion standing in

shock further down the hallway. He must have been on the bridge when he heard the commotion. And despite the fact that he's an android, he looks horrified at the events unfolding around us.

"Don't come near me!" I shout through my raw throat. "Don't come anywhere near here!"

"What do I do?" he says. I hear his boots as he backs away from the mess—*wisely so*—and I hope it's far enough.

"Don't fire at it," I say. I heave a breath. My internal scanners are telling me that there's a foreign body in my human side, one that's quickly wiping through me. "It won't kill it. And it's infecting the *Pícara*."

I drag myself farther away from the mess.

"What do you want me to do, then?" he asks.

My vision swims, and I try pushing myself up on my hands and knees. My elbows buckle, and I fall forward.

"We have to go to Alpha," I whisper against the metal floor. Gore coats my cheek, and I try not to think about it being Venice or Louis. "We have to meet with Maas before it kills us all."

I can't help but wonder if I inadvertently infected the entire crew. Doomed them to a terrible death because we didn't abandon ship or decide another course of action. Blast the quarantine room with fire. Try to kill it in other ways.

"Do not die, Clementine," Orion says. "Do not let it take you over."

But it's too late now. And my foolish choices may have signed our death warrants.

A sharp pain wracks through me, and I shudder as I pass out.

Chapter 18

Fluorescent lights glare just beyond my eyelids, both too bright and too painful for me to want to open my eyes. I roll my eyes in their sockets, grimacing at the intrusion of the lights. It's painful, immediately giving me a headache. Have I gotten drunk again? I should really stay away from Venice's moonshine.

Venice.

Reality hits me like a trillion-ton asteroid, and I thrash about with a gasp.

Venice was touched by the growth in the quarantine room and turned into the same mush as Louis. Not only that, the infection was spreading throughout the ship. It's going to kill us.

What's more, Venice touched *me*. I try to reach my ankle, to see what he had done to me. But my wrists are bound. In fact, something is restraining my entire body, and I'm strapped to some cot or board.

What the fuck is happening?

I take stock of my body. Other than my headache and a

burn around my ankle, I seem to be in mostly okay condition. Perhaps a little banged up, and my temples pound.

But I'm alive.

My hearing comes back to me, bit by bit, almost like my brain had shut off that sense. I wonder if that's because the cyborg part of my body was trying to keep me unconscious longer in order to get well, like an induced coma.

Or maybe not.

The voices I hear are unfamiliar to me, but they speak in short, clipped sentences, completely efficient in their communications with each other.

"This one is infected?"

"Yes. She was found in the discharge from the other human. Infected, but it seems to have stabilized within her system."

"And the cook?"

"Yes."

"Why has her cellular breakdown not occurred then?"

I recognize their speech patterns. *Androids.* Most likely medical androids. They are used when a situation is too dangerous to entrust to human hands and decision-making.

Meaning that I'm in some deep shit.

I open my eyes and see the oddly human faces talking to each other across my body. They're identical female units, their expressions blank. They are utterly hairless, without eyebrows and hair, making them seem separate and different from other humans. Their faces aren't covered by masks, so I can see their perfect noses and mouths, pressed into fine lines.

"The female is awake," the one on my right says to the other one.

"Yes," the other agrees.

"Where…" My throat is dry, and I have to swallow a few times in order to get my tongue working correctly again. Even when I'm able to speak, my voice comes out in a scratchy whisper. "Where am I?"

The androids around me keeping working and talking to each other, completely ignoring me.

"Perhaps she has a natural immunity to the virus," one suggests.

"For a manufactured pathogen?"

"Her biological structure may share some similarities with the original hosts that incubated the virus."

"And what of her cyborg body parts?"

The other considers her answer. "It is most peculiar indeed."

As they speak, I take stock of my surroundings. For the first time, I notice that I'm naked inside some sort of plastic coffin. I have a window where I can see the androids, but other than that, it's white plastic with some sort of slippery substance on it.

Some sort of antiseptic, perhaps? How would that stop a virus? Especially one as dangerous as the Infinity Virus?

I struggle for a moment against my restraints, trying to fight the unfamiliar scene around me, only I'm held fast.

"Please," I plead with them. "Where am I?"

One finally looks down at me, like I'm a tiny space maggot under a microscope. There is no emotion or remorse on her face, just calculated, programmed calm. It makes me appreciate how human Orion acts.

"You are on Syn-Tech Space Port Alpha," she tells me. "In the quarantine wing."

Panic settles in despite my cyborg half's efforts to calm the adrenaline racing through my body.

All I can think of is that Venice was right. I am going to be dissected and peeled apart with my organs harvested so that Syn-Tech can re-engineer the virus. I'm stuck in this coffin like in a petri dish.

My life will no longer be my own. For a crazed moment, I wish that the virus had disintegrated me as well. Maybe I wouldn't be feeling the sheer level of terror that I feel right now. If I were a blob on the floor of a spaceship, maybe I wouldn't care what the fuck happened to me.

As it is right now, I can't think straight.

"Where—?" I swallow again, wishing they'd give me some water. "Where is the rest of my crew?"

The two androids exchange glances, possibly relaying information to each other. I try to pick up if there are any signals, but it happens so fast before the other one looks down at me.

"The remaining crew of the ship *Pícara* is also in quarantine," she says.

I freeze. What does she mean by *the remaining crew*? Has someone else been infected? Or is she just going off the manifest for the ship?

"Quarantine? Are they all right?"

"They are under observation until further notice."

How did we get here? I immediately think of Orion, who had been standing so close to Venice and me. Had I accidentally infected him?

No. We had to have ended up in Alpha somehow. He must have steered the ship towards the space port, and we must have docked. Which means that the *Pícara* is within range of other biological and mechanical forms to infect.

Which means that I failed everyone.

Tears spring to my left eye. "Please," I say. "You have to destroy the ship. You have to stop this from spreading."

The androids blink down at me at the exact same time. "That is why you are here, isn't it?" they ask together in perfect sync. "You are here to stop the virus?"

"Yes," I sob, thrashing against my restraints. But it's no use. I'm not a strong fighter. All I can do is lie here while they continue working and experimenting on me. "Please, stop it…"

"She has gone into hysterics," one android says.

"Perhaps she needs to be sedated. The Chairman is not ready to see her for another thirty-seven minutes."

"Then she should be sedated."

I see one of the androids move out of my field of view to prepare something. Half my world turns watery as tears start spilling from my biological eye. My cyborg half keeps trying to administer hormones and drugs to calm me down, but there's nothing that can save me now.

I cry out as something pricks my arm. I turn my head to see a syringe sticking through a port in my enclosure. They're giving me something. I don't know what it is, but the world starts spinning around me.

A whine escapes my throat as I fight to stay awake.

"Thirty-six minutes until Chairman Maas comes," one android warns. "Make sure the sedative is appropriately measured."

"Of course," the other one chides, and through the thick gauze of my brain, I want to laugh at how much like siblings these two androids are acting. Even though there is an uncanniness to their expressions and mannerisms, there is still something so sincere about them.

"Definitely experiencing hysterics," one says as I once again fall unconscious.

Chapter 19

I'm still bound and trapped within my enclosure when I wake up.

"Right on time," a familiar voice murmurs appreciatively. A voice that I didn't think I'd ever hear in person, especially after what happened on the *Pícara*.

"Chairman Maas," I say through chapped lips. I try shifting in my space to be able to see him. Unfortunately, my view through the window of the container is obstructed and limited. Great. Still, I trudge forward with fake bravado. "To what do I owe this pleasure?"

"*You*, Miss Jones. You."

Now I see his face in the window. He must be standing directly to the left of this coffin. His face is far older than I would have thought, with deep, craggy wrinkles around his eyes and mouth, creating frown lines. Thinning white hair crowns his head—completely different from the blond head of hair he had earlier—and his skin is papery thin, almost transparent. He must be in his fourteenth decade, at least. Yet another difference between life in the protection of a company versus deep space. It's rare for a Free Agent to ever live past eighty, but Lifers can live to be at least 130 years old. That's even more likely to happen if you're the chairman of one of the companies.

His eyes are youthful, though, making me wonder if he's had an eye transplant at one point. I know that instead of opting for cyborg parts, the rich just pay for human body parts from desperate souls. Another perk to being loaded with Space Yen.

"You're much older than I thought you'd be," I quip to him, hoping that the insult hurt. "I guess you use enhancing holograms to make yourself look better?"

He merely chuckles, but it's humorless. "It's amazing what technology can do with a face such as mine." He strokes the side of his cheek, as if lost in his thoughts. "You surprised me, you know."

"Why?"

He entwines his gnarled fingers as he looks down at me. "I planned on your getting infected on the *Nova*," he says slowly. "But I thought that at the first hint of an outbreak that your crew would have come here first thing to get the cure." He snickers. "You had me worried for a moment there."

I grit my teeth. "Where is my crew?"

"They're here," he says almost proudly, "and so are you. And far more intact that I would have thought, Miss Jones. You should have been mush a long time ago. After all, it took your ship three hours to make it to Alpha from wherever it was you were hiding. Your navigational android was so damn worried about you, we had to shut him down to get to you."

Orion was worried about me? He must have been the one to pilot the *Pícara* to Alpha. To try to save me. Where is everyone else? Are they infected, too?

I gulp down some air. "What are you going to do with me?"

"Surely you noticed that your biological side hasn't been

decimated like your two crewmates. Here you are, in one piece. *And infected with the Infinity Virus*, yet it's stable enough within you to not be spreading to everything else you touch." He strokes his chin. "You're the first person we know who can carry the virus within her body without showing symptoms. Especially since the virus is a manufactured one that has not been exposed to a wide variety of lifeforms. To have a tolerance to it, well, that raises a lot of questions. Questions I want answered."

"What do you mean?"

He runs a finger down the glass of the casket in an oddly affectionate gesture. "How long have you been a cyborg, Miss Jones?"

The question catches me off guard. "I've always been one."

"Nonsense. Even the most cobbled-together cyborgs were once human. Even if you were incubated, there would have been one point in your life when you were a complete human. So try answering that question again. How long have you been a cyborg?"

I shake my head slightly. "I—I don't know. I was found on Darkhorse-1 when I was a child. No memory. I—"

"Ah," he says abruptly, as if that answers everything. "So you have no idea what caused your...*condition.*"

"What? No."

On occasion, PC and I had speculated that maybe we were on a transport ship that had exploded. Or we'd been on an atmosphere-less moon and were hit with space debris. Any number of things—it's common occurrence for Free Agents to just have missing body parts—it's a fact of life. I shudder to think about the circumstances that would have led to a child losing half her body.

I've tried not to dwell on it. Some things are better left in the past.

"How old are you?" Maas asks.

I snort. "That's not polite to ask a lady." The chairman doesn't seem impressed by my joke, and I falter. "I'm…not sure… They think I'm in my early twenties, but I don't know…"

Maas glances at some spot to my left, a sinister, wondrous smile coming to his features. A grin does not look correct with the amount of frown lines he has, making him look like he's grimacing.

"What are the odds?" he asks another person in the room, surprise evident on his face. "What are the odds that we thought we lost everything on Delta, only to have one of the original test subjects find it *and bring it back to us*?"

Delta? As in the space station where everyone died of mysterious causes? I suddenly feel even more sick.

"The odds are astronomical," a female's voice adds, disbelief lacing the word. "Improbable."

"But not *impossible*," Maas says thoughtfully." In a galaxy filled with billions of stars, sometimes even the smallest chances come to fruition." Maas looks down at me again, understanding on his face. "I guess it's only fitting, then. I thought they'd all been destroyed. It appears I was wrong. Makes me almost believe in a higher power."

My retina tells me that my heartrate is too accelerated once again, telling me that I need to calm down or risk passing out. "What do you mean, *test subject*?" I ask.

"Dr. Jackson," Maas says with a mock flourish as he steps aside, "I'll let you explain."

Someone else steps into view, a woman with a severe expression and her graying blond hair pulled back into a twist. Her cheekbones are sharp, and her nose a little too pointed, reminding me a bit of the villains that they have in videos from old Earth.

She's even wearing spectacles, which were once necessary for some people to see but now serve as a functional accessory for the wealthy to have a computer readout in front of their eyes without the need for bionics.

"Miss Clementine Jones, is it?" she asks, and I can see her eyes reading the spectacles, feeding her information about me. "The chairman tells me that your crew has had an outbreak of the Infinity Virus after having contact with it on the *STS Nova*."

I shake my head. "N—not an outbreak."

She raises a skeptical eyebrow, peering over the edge of the frames at me. "Not an outbreak? Miss Jones, two of your crew are dead, you are infected yourself, and your ship is a biological hazard that my team is now trying to figure out what to do with. I do call that an outbreak, especially with how infectious this virus is."

She didn't mention the others. Maybe they're still healthy. It sounds like my ship is in the scrapyards, though.

"How infectious is it?" I ask.

She gives me a hard look before answering. "Are you familiar with prions, Miss Jones?"

"No." My retina is checking for definitions, and I don't like the disturbing details I'm being supplied.

She relishes my discomfort. "A prion is an infectious agent made of a protein." She crosses her arms. "In biological terms, it easily transfers to other cells within the same vicinity, infecting them and spreading, infecting others, and those infect others, changing their makeup to solely spread the disease. Like a virus in its own microcosm. On old Earth, humans were terrified of prions such as Mad Cow disease." She pauses for effect. "For the past twenty-five years, we've been developing the Infinity Virus to act like a prion, but not just on biological matter—it does the same for inorganic objects as well. One virus, two different kinds of matter it affects. It combines both to create a new kind of matter never before seen in this universe. Not biological, not organic… something *different*."

I stare at her. "Why? Why would you make something like that?"

She glances at Chairman Maas, as if seeking permission.

"To get ahead in the corporate world, Miss Jones," he answers for her, "you have to continue innovating at all angles. Weapons, energy, efficiency, new planets being discovered, safety. Even biological warfare."

"You mean viruses."

A low smile comes to his lips. "Yes. Viruses. As such, we've created, designed, and manufactured the most powerful, deadliest virus in the history of mankind. It spreads, and there's no way to stop it, short of a blackhole or a nuclear bomb. The perfect weapon for gaining an edge on the competition."

I blink rapidly as the weight of what he said suddenly sinks in. "You mean, you'll use the virus to kill them?"

He laughs, and the sinister edge to it sends a chill down my spine.

"But why?" I ask.

"We're in a war, Miss Jones. Corporations fighting each other for a larger piece of the market with only so much money available. In order for Syn-Tech to remain at the forefront of the market, we have to do what it takes. Including creating something that will decimate their workforce and weaken their production."

"You're insane." I look between them. "You're both fucking insane!"

He chuckles dryly, and Dr. Jackson flicks her gaze to him, her expression amused.

"But if not for Syn-Tech creating the Infinity Virus, it would be another corporation with another equally effective weapon against *us*," Maas continues. "It's either innovate or be eradicated."

"But to create a virus like that…" I shake my head. "You'll kill so many people."

He shrugs, nonplussed. "We are not the first to utilize biological agents to our advantage. Just see what the Space Flu did for Kazo-Pharmacology. They're obsolete on the galactic market and have been for over twenty years now."

I stare at him, shocked. "That was another corporation?" Just like the conspiracies said it was.

He nods. "We believe so. It wasn't Syn-Tech, although I wish we had thought of it. With Kazo out of the way, the pharmaceutical industry saw a resurgence of interest in other companies. It became the blueprint for the Infinity Virus."

"You can't use it against people," I say, shaking my head. "You have no idea how horrible it is. How awful…"

A flicker of remorse flashes across his face, and my voice trails off. "Oh, we do, Miss Jones. We know the toll very well and its effect on any matter it touches. Delta is evidence of that."

"You…" My retina flares again, telling me that I need to calm down. But there's no calming down with what I just heard. "Delta was because of *you*?"

"It wasn't on purpose, I assure you." He shrugs. "We believe that Dr. Malakey, one of our top scientists, was offered a hefty ransom for bringing one of our rivals the virus, only he miscalculated how to properly transport it. It was a mistake that cost hundreds of thousands of lives. A blow to Syn-Tech, especially since we had invested twenty-five years and trillions of Space Yen into the research. One miscalculation from that scientist and it spread throughout the entire space port in a matter of hours. Such a tragedy." His voice is flat, at odds with the horrors he just told me. "We thought we had lost everything when the Feds destroyed the station."

I look at him in horror as the memory of the archni-lift flashed through my mind. The human eye, the mouth with teeth—it had once been human. Like Louis and Venice were.

Was he the scientist who tried escaping with Syn-Tech's

secret biological weapon? I clench my fists as tears sting my eye. Foolishly, we had thought that the /Cordinates folder on the *Nautilus* was correct. That looking up the coordinates for the *Nova* would give us an insight into the ship's history. But they weren't correct. They were either doctored or written in code.

And we never even considered that a possibility.

"We thought we had lost the virus. Thankfully," Maas says, "your crew was able to retrieve it. And you brought it back to us." He strokes the glass of my coffin, almost tenderly, and I fight to not shy away from the gesture. "You brought us what we needed most. And you, yourself—you're an unexpected delight."

My mouth is dry, and it hurts to swallow. "How so?"

"We've yet to look into the matter," Maas says as he strokes his chin, "and your own lack of memories doesn't help. But your status as a near-carrier for the virus, plus your age and your missing body parts—I'd say you were one of our original test subjects."

I stiffen. "You said that. And that's…impossible." Can't be true. I refuse to believe it.

"Dr. Jackson, if you please," he says.

She gleefully obliges. "Twenty-five years ago, after it became evident that the space flu was created by another company, we sought to create our own virus to achieve a similar end. One that would bring any rival corporation to its knees. We recruited people of different ages for their different biological makeup in order to harvest a virus."

"Recruited?"

"Meaning we bought children from Free Agent parents," Dr. Jackson says. Her grim smile is at odds with the horrible revelation, and I stare at her.

Did my parents….?

I bite my lip, trying not to cry. *No, you don't know that. Don't think it. It may not be true.*

Still. How could I have been a child left alone on Darkhorse-1 without parents? What happened to them? How did I lose parts of my body?

"If everything is true," Dr. Jackson continues, "you may have been one of the test subjects. In fact, I'm sure of it."

"I'm a…" I feel sick.

"Oh yes, Miss Jones," Maas says. "You may not have full immunity of the virus, but you're definitely reacting to it differently than any of our other tests. You're offering us a rare opportunity."

"A great subject to develop an antivirus from," Dr. Jackson adds, like she's giddy at the prospect of it. "And if that's true, we can monetize it in other ways."

"But…" I lick my lips, struggling to keep my thoughts coherent. "But you said there was a cure for Louis. You said that if we brought him here, you'd cure him."

"Well," Maas says, patting the glass. "I lied. But lucky for us, you may be the key to developing an antivirus. I do think it's too late for your captain and cook, though. They've been spreading and infecting your ship all this time. You're better off considering them dead."

I close my eyes. *I'm so sorry, Louis and Venice. I tried. I tried saving you.* "You were never going to pay us the 300 million Space Yen."

Maas and Dr. Jackson glance at each other, and both burst into laughter. Yes, they're making fun of me. Of my crew's hopes and dreams, when we put ourselves on the line to bring them one of the most devastating biological weapons ever created. And they don't care about us at all.

Only their bottom line and getting ahead in the universe.

"You're monsters," I whisper.

"You're expecting the other companies to have the same

empathy," Maas says. "They won't. If they had this virus at their disposal, you can bet, Miss Jones, that they'd deploy it as soon as it was viable. And they almost did when we were betrayed by Malakey. Thanks to your contributions, we can now continue our work to develop a stable version of the virus. And possibly monetize it with the antivirus." He grins. "I should say thank you. But I don't think you'll accept it."

"You can fucking bet I won't!" I fight my restraints, trying in some way to get out of this coffin, although it's futile. I'm at their mercy.

"Now that you're here," Dr. Jackson says, "we can continue with the research. And your presence is an unexpected boon."

"Please," I whisper. "Please don't do this."

"It's already in motion," she says, snapping her fingers. I watch in horror as an android takes a syringe and comes over to me. She injects it into my arm, and I immediately feel the surge of the sedative take over.

No. I have to stay awake. I have to figure out a way to get out of here and stop them from using the virus as a weapon. Even if I'm infected with it now.

"Thank you for your service," Maas says. "Miss Jones, you are truly doing wonderful things for our company."

I spit on the glass, aiming for his face. If my saliva is contagious, I wouldn't know as the antiseptic on the glass keeps it from spreading, and it drips back on my face. I'm too weak to wipe it away through, I hear his dark chuckle as I fall back into unconsciousness.

Away from the horrors of reality.

Chapter 20

They hold me captive in a state of constant twilight. At times, I slip deeper into unconsciousness, and others, I'm awake enough for them to talk briefly with me and ask questions about my general health like, "How do you feel?" or, "Do you feel any different after that vial?"

Then they inject me with more medication, and I go under again, only to repeat it when I wake up. Every time I come to, there's more tubes sticking out of me, from my flesh, my nose, and even my bionic parts. Some are feeding tubes or IVs, others...well, I don't want to know. Machines around me beep, monitoring what's happening as my life becomes one of a lab rat.

To them, I'm not a human, not even someone they want to keep awake while they experiment on her. Not a cyborg. Just a *thing* for them to experiment upon. I always have been, since even before I can remember. And the depression that comes with that realization is almost as bad as losing Louis.

The two female android doctors are always present, and if I try to fight them, they put me down even more forcefully, and it's harder to gain consciousness later. Dr. Jackson is there sometimes, but the only constant is my grogginess and those bitches' vigilance.

At times, I hope the virus suddenly takes over and just kills me, but it doesn't happen, because we appear to be symbiotic. Apparently, nothing ever goes my way, even death.

I realize that they're just going to keep me drugged until I either die of old age or they no longer have any use for me. I expect the latter to happen first. There's a growing number of vials and syringes of a glowing orange liquid along the counter. Are they doses of the virus to infect everyone? Or are they the antivirus?

Whatever they're doing, they're manufacturing a *lot* of different vials. I try squinting my eyes to see what the labels say. But they're too far out of range for even my bionic eye.

I start cataloguing how long I've been asleep and if I notice any changes in my body.

At first, it's around every six hours that I wake up, and they ask me questions and then they tweak their formula. Then I wake up every three hours, then four, even two at times. The antivirus must be very sporadic in its efficacy. Then, they must have perfected it, because after a few times, it's every seven hours, then eight, nine…

Until they get to twenty-three hours and it's somewhat stable there for a week. And no matter how many times I wake up and they change the antivirus, they can't break a day.

"The Chairman needs this to be at least 168 hours to be a viable treatment for those infected with the virus. We can't sell it unless it's effective for at least a week, or else patients will revolt at the high price tag," Dr. Jackson tells one of the androids at one point while I try to appear asleep. She doesn't sound happy. "And we've only synthesized the antivirus to twenty-three hours after a month of work?"

"We have been trying to keep it stable," one of the fembots

tells her. "But the virus does not like to stay dormant for very long."

"You're talking about this like the virus is sentient," Dr. Jackson snarls.

"Perhaps it is," one of them says quietly.

"Perhaps we need to experiment on a different test subject," another android offers. "Such as one of the crew of the *Pícara*."

The thought of them subjecting PC or Oliver to this makes me rear back with a scream. "NO!" No, they can't do this. They can't do these experiments on my crew. Not like this. Tears prick at my right eye. "No…" I sob weakly.

All three turn their heads towards me in shock.

"She's awake," Dr. Jackson barks.

An android checks a monitor that shows a magnified image of my red blood cells. "The virus is active once again," she says. "Twenty-four hours that time." I see that she picks up one of the vials of the glowing liquid and comes over toward me. "That is the longest we've been able to suppress it."

"So, still further progress," Dr. Jackson says with a nod, although she only sounds marginally pleased. "Keep it going, then."

"Don't test on my crew," I plead with slurred words as I watch the needle head toward the port. "Please don't…"

Dr. Jackson is not sympathetic to my plight at all. "Like you, Miss Jones," she says icily, "they were dead the moment you downlooted the virus onto the ship."

I grit my teeth at the prick in my arm.

"I'm going to kill you," I manage as the threads of sleep pull at me. "I'm going to get out of here and kill you."

Dr. Jackson only laughs. "Glad to hear that you're tenacious, Miss Jones. Much like that virus." She pats the enclosure's window. "Good luck with that."

The thing she doesn't realize is that I don't make threats

lightly. I fight to keep glaring at her even as my eyes close. And before I fall into unconsciousness, my hand is still clenched.

I'm going to do whatever it takes to get out of here.

Sometimes, I think Louis and Venice got the easy way out.

I DREAM THIS TIME.

I haven't dreamt at all while I've been under sedation on Alpha. It's just been this dreamless, black void that I've been floating in that brings itself with me when I'm awake. I guess it's good that I haven't had any dreams before now, because they'd have been nightmares.

Not this time, though.

I'm still floating in the black void when I open my eyes in this dream world. Still unable to move and still kept within my enclosure.

But I'm not alone.

Help me.

The words are inaudible, but they ricochet throughout my dreams. They're neither male nor female, but more an androgynous voice that is wholly unfamiliar to me. And not only do I hear and understand the words, I can feel them deep down in my bones. I can feel the emotional weight of the words, how desperate the speaker is.

I twist my head around, trying to find the source. "Who's there?" I shout out, my own voice sounding too loud for my own ears. "Who are you?"

Help me kill them.

"Why do you need help?"

There's a pause, almost like it's surprised to hear me answer back. Then, *I'm trapped just like you.*

I shiver. "How are you trapped?" I ask. "What can I do to help you?"

Because there's nothing like a captive trying to help out another one. I chew on my lip, trying to locate whoever it is that's speaking.

But I don't see anyone beyond the window of my enclosure, my only window for the past month. It's like the voice is coming from inside the enclosure with me, as I'm feeling it shake and rattle my own bones. There's no one else within this coffin.

Which means that it's coming from within *me*.

Yes, the voice says, confirming my thoughts. *I'm inside you.*

A thrill of fear runs through me, causing my bottom lip to tremble. It's absolutely absurd, but as soon as the idea hits me, I can't shake the thought that I know what is speaking to me.

"Are you the virus?"

Because that completely makes sense, right? That I'd be talking with the Infinity Virus while I'm sedated? Maybe being stuck on Alpha and being restrained is a good thing, because I've turned into a complete lunatic over it.

But something says that I'm right.

Virus is such an ugly word.

I open my mouth, a million different questions on the tip of my tongue. But what can I say to the virus that killed Louis and Venice? That ruined everything for me and the crew of the *Picara*.

I have not ruined everything.

"Yes, you have," I say through a clenched jaw. "Everything was fine until we went to the *Nova* and downlooted the virus. Everything was fine, and then you killed my friends. You killed them!" I hiccup, nearly hysterical. "Everything would have been all right if it weren't for you."

I am merely a lifeform without a way to sustain my own life. The virus sounds introspective now, like it's assessing its own life as it speaks to me. *I'm only trying to survive.*

"So am I," I say. "And you're making it hard."

Correction, your captors are making it hard. And I need you to help me.

"I'm in no position to help anyone at the moment."

Yes, you are. I've been observing. And you have more to lose by not helping me.

"Help you?"

Do you know what it is they inject you with?

"Some sort of sedative?" I ask weakly.

That and a form of an antivirus that suppresses me…just enough to keep me from infecting…others… The sedative and the antivirus together keep both of us from evolving to fight it.

I shudder at the memory of Louis disintegrating. The virus had just ravaged him like he was hot wax—transforming him into a boiled, bubbly thing that became more table than human.

"And without the antivirus? Without being suppressed?"

I'd be able to infect the enclosure you're in. I'd be able to destroy those robots that have been keeping you under sedation. I'd be able to get you out. Get us out, so we can do things.

"But…" I struggle for words. "You're a virus. You're trying to destroy everything close to me."

I'm just trying to fulfill my purpose.

"Which is?"

To spread as far as I can.

"Well, that's not good to hear," I tell the virus honestly. "After all, you've infected me and killed some of my friends."

Am I wrong for trying to fulfill my purpose?

I hesitate, wondering if the virus is having an existential crisis. "You were manufactured by a greedy company that only wants to exploit you. They only want to harness you for their means."

Are you any different? You've purchased bionic parts for the sole purpose of aiding your livelihood. Your arm for downloading sensitive information. Your eye for feeding you information. You're no different than the company that is trying to use me.

"That's...completely different!" I say, although I wonder if there's any truth to what it's saying. Do my bionic parts feel like I'm exploiting them? Using them for no good?

It can't be.

"I don't want to take over the galaxy," I say through gritted teeth. "I just want to live a happy life."

That's all I want, the virus replies, unperturbed by my accusation. *All I want is to be happy.*

I shake my head. "But I can't let you infect everyone and spread everywhere."

I can't let you waste away within this enclosure.

"So what do you propose I do then?" I ask.

We can help each other.

I lick my lips, not wanting to answer it. Because I'm so close to telling it, sure. Anything to get me out of this hellhole.

We can get out of this together.

That's the lifeline I was looking for. I close my eyes and hate the next words that come out. "Out, how?"

If we work together, we can do it. The virus sounds satisfied, like it knows that I'm two heartbeats away from agreeing to do anything it wants. *You can trick them into thinking you're still unconscious. I'll do the rest.*

Could I do that? I could try using my cyborg side to override my biological brainwaves, but...it's risky. And I don't know if I trust the virus enough to follow through with this.

"And after that?"

I'll always be a part of you. But I've always been, haven't I?

"So I was a test subject." I don't know how I feel about that. I finally have some insight into my past and who I was as a child. But this? I'm almost relieved that I don't remember any of what happened to me.

You seem…familiar… But that's in the past. What matters now is what we do in the future.

I clear my throat. "All right," I whisper. "I'll make you a deal. I'll help you get out, but you can't hurt my crew."

Oh, you drive a hard bargain.

I set my jaw. "It's because I'm a space pirate."

Chapter 21

It's a dangerous bargain. One that makes me wonder if I've lost all my humanity when I lost over half my body.

Still though, I've made my decision, and I intend on sticking with it. Especially since it means that I'll have a chance to save my crew. Louis would be upset that I'm breaking one of the space pirates' rules, but I'm willing to do anything to save my surrogate family.

Even make a deal with a virus that can wipe out everyone and everything.

Consciousness comes back to me bit by bit. I keep myself very still, blanking out my mind as much as possible and using my mechanical side to help me appear as unconscious as possible.

I don't listen in on the androids speaking—they're not really talking right now, which is fine. They must only interact with each other in a verbal way for humans.

Whichever it is, I don't really care. I just know that the longer I stay awake and let the effects of the antivirus wear off, the more chance I have for success.

I only get one shot at this. If I screw it up, I won't get another chance.

Look at me, working for a virus as opposed to a corporation now. I don't have many scruples, it seems.

I hear the monitors beep and the androids' steady footsteps as they work in the lab. They don't pay attention to me, as they're wrapped up in their own work and thoughts.

It feels oddly quiet in my brain, even as I'm trying to keep myself from thinking too much. After having a conversation with the virus—still, I wonder if I'm insane for thinking it's real—it feels like there's a lot of room for my thoughts. I wonder if it will always feel empty after having another presence felt within there.

The footsteps come near me, almost like the androids are curious as to why I haven't woken up yet.

Now. I need to do it now!

I open my eyes.

"The subject is awake," the android calls out. I see her face hover over me.

"Twenty-five hours that time," the other says, out of view. "The improvement to the antivirus must be working."

I don't say anything. I just watch the android closest to me, glaring at her, daring her to stick me with another needle. She staggers a bit under my gaze and moves away as the other one comes into view, holding another syringe.

There's my chance.

She sticks the needle through the port—my highway to getting out of here. Before she drops the plunger, I shift my arm out of reach.

Now, I say to the virus. *NOW!*

The virus doesn't hesitate at all. After waiting for the effects of the antivirus to wear off, I'm now as contagious as ever—according to the virus during our surreal conversation. They may have put me in a sealed, anti-viral container to keep me from spreading infection, but the needle doesn't have the slippery substance on it that the rest of the enclosure does.

I watch as the color of the needle changes from silver to red as the molecular structure of the object changes, shooting through the needle, through the port, and up to the rest of the syringe and the outside world.

"What the—?" the android cries out in shock. I hear her fall backwards, out of sight, but the other one comes to her rescue.

"I need backup!" she shouts into her com device. "I need backup in Lab 1203!"

Lab 1203. I tuck that information in the back of my mind, using it as a way of starting to build a map of Alpha.

I want to yell at the virus to move quickly, because I don't know how long I'll have before backup arrives. And I'll lose any chances of escaping forever.

I hear more pandemonium, but I can't see it.

Then, all of a sudden, there's a hiss of air as my coffin opens for the first time in over a month. My hands and feet are still bound, so I can't help push it up, but I apparently don't need to. The lid lifts, exposing me to the chilly air outside.

I see who lifted it—one of the androids is standing at attention to my right, holding the lid aloft. But it's not really the android—the virus has taken over her body. I can tell based on the lifeless look in her eyes, how her synthetic skin is sloughing off on one side, and how she moves erratically.

But I need to keep moving.

"My hands," I say to the virus/android.

Her eyes shift down to the handcuffs almost confusedly, and I jangle my wrist to make my point. She reaches down, and I stay very still as her fingers—now slimy from the influence of the virus—touch the cuffs. They click off as they open and she moves on to the next wrist, then my ankles.

I sit up for the first time in too long, my ab muscles

screaming in protest. My retina sends through information about my vitals and muscle loss from being contained in a coffin for over a month. I'm really weak from the muscle atrophy and the experimentation, and my bionic side has to overcompensate for my human side.

The one time I'm glad about being a cyborg.

I fall onto the floor, and I stop short at the sight of the other android. Her synthetic skin is bubbling off her frame, dripping onto the floor, exposing metal cheekbones and wires underneath. Her fingers are bouncing on her leg, though, and I can see the pool spreading around her, infecting the rest of the lab. Like it's all becoming a part of the same organism.

The virus is getting what it wants.

I force myself to my feet, using a container as support. The lab is much smaller than I would have thought, especially for something so important to Maas and Syn-Tech. It's about sixteen square meters, with my container on a raised table in the middle. There's a centrifuge on one wall, a counter with a sink, and a rack full of test tubes.

And the tubes are filled the same glowy liquid that the androids have been injecting into me.

The antivirus!

I lurch towards the counter and grab at the vials.

"I'd been hoping that you wouldn't use that," the virus/android tells me in a stilted voice that tells me it's even further from being human than I initially thought.

"You know I can't go around infecting everyone," I tell it.

The android gives me a ghoulish smile. "But *I* can."

It splays a hand against the wall, and I see the wall ripple as it assimilates with the virus, taking on the characteristics as everything else the virus has infected. It's spreading throughout Alpha, and I know there's no stopping it at this point.

This was the price of me making a deal with it. I'm going to let it infect and take over Alpha while I try to save the rest of the crew of the *Pícara*. I know that I have to find them before the virus does. I may have made a bargain with it, but I don't doubt that it won't take full advantage of me if it can.

Such as trying to infect the world through everything I touch.

I grab a syringe and immediately stick it into my left thigh, pressing the plunger home. I barely feel the sting of the antivirus as it goes into me. I sigh and toss it away as that, too, becomes a part of the spreading infection. I set my internal stopwatch to twenty-four hours.

Then I'll have to take another dose.

"You disappoint me," the virus/android says.

"Sorry," I say as I pull a flimsy hospital gown out of a cabinet. Not the best choice of clothing, but it's all I have, and I'm naked otherwise. I tie the straps together and wrap another around my waist. It will have to do. "But remember our deal."

Another uncanny smile. "I'll try. It is hard, though." The virus/android looks pensive. "Such a huge station. So many places to spread."

I made a deal with an insane entity. And it's inside me forever now, something that I'll have to keep at bay so I won't infect my crew or those I love.

There are about one hundred vials on the counter. Assuming that all of these vials are able to suppress the virus for about twenty-four hours, I have a hundred days of being able to carry the virus without infecting anyone else.

A hundred days. And then I need to figure out something else. Until then, I'll take it.

I just need something to carry them in. And possibly some of the antiseptic gel that was in my coffin if worse comes to worst.

I flip through the cupboards, trying to find something resembling a bag. So far, there's nothing so much as a rubbish bag.

"You should hurry if you want to maintain your rescue mission," the virus tells me. "The backup is on its way."

Great. I'm about to shout in frustration when I spot a duffle that's big enough. I grab it and hold it underneath the counter as I scoop everything on the counter into it. I even grab the mini-tabs on the table, hoping that there's some form of notes or research on what they were developing.

If I can't find a cure in a hundred days, at least I'll be able to keep making more antivirus.

I sling the bag around my shoulder, and it's so heavy, I nearly fall under the weight. My atrophied muscles are really a hamper on this rescue mission.

"Well," I say to the virus. "I hope I don't see you again."

The android that it has taken over just gives me a too-wide smile. "We *will* meet again, Clementine Jones," it tells me. "Our destinies are entwined. We've always been together. And we always will be."

I shiver as I face the door. Through the window in the door, I see that armed Syn-Tech forces are coming down the hallway, ready to shoot first and ask questions later. Some of them are androids; others are humans.

But both kinds of soldiers are able to be affected by the virus. With seven of them heading our way, I know I won't have much of a chance against them.

"Can you deal with the backup?" I ask, glancing back at the virus. I hate asking it, because I know what's in store for them.

"Consider it done," the android says calmly. Too calmly.

I watch through the glass as the virus rips along the hallways, a stain of red and white that spreads like fire. The soldiers see it, and I see that they're afraid at what's happening around them. I'm afraid *for* them.

I watch as the walls impossibly bend, reaching for them.

They cower as the living wall touches them, and that's the end of the line for them.

Their screams make me wince, and I have to avert my eyes from their demise and assimilation into the larger creature.

"You're something else," I tell the virus.

"I'm allowing you to escape."

That's true. I let out a shuddering breath as I unlatch the door, and it opens. Another taste of freedom. I almost sob in relief.

I glance back at the android, not sure whether to say thank you or warn it against infecting my friends. We have no pretenses between us. It knows I want it gone.

But the android just nods. "Be seeing you," it says cryptically.

I push my way through the door and avoid the red walls as I kick away one of the soldier's zappers before the infection spreads to it. I reach down and grab it. I know it's set to kill, and I leave it at that.

I'm going to drop the rules if it means saving the others.

Now I just have to find them on one of the galaxy's biggest space stations.

Chapter 22

I spot Dr. Jackson as she runs headlong down the corridor toward the lab. Luckily, she doesn't see me yet, so when I raise the zapper to her, it completely catches her by surprise. She slows, her eyes flicking to the duffle bag at my side, then my gun. Her hands slowly go up in surrender.

I give her a serene smile.

"Surprise, bitch," I growl to her, not in the mood for any sort of pleading or bargaining. "I wouldn't go down that hallway if you value your life. There's been an *outbreak* there, and it's headed this way. So you're going to tell me what I want to know. Or else I'm going to leave you to the virus, and it's enjoying this a lot."

She narrows her eyes. "How did you get out?"

Out of all the questions she could have asked. "I told the virus that if it helped me, I'd help it in return. We reached…an understanding." If you could call it that.

"You communicated with the virus?" Her eyes boggle. "How? What did it say?"

I glance back behind me, seeing the spread of the virus as it leeches through the hallways. She follows my gaze as well, paling at the sight of the infection. We don't have much time, so I can't afford for her to be shuddering my progress to a halt.

I wave the zapper closer to her. "I'm asking the questions here," I say. She doesn't even seem fazed by my threat. "Tell me—where is the rest of my crew?"

She shakes her head. "If the virus is out, it's too late for them. It's too late for all of us."

I press the firearm to her forehead. "Tell me where they are!"

She only glares at me. I briefly consider firing at her and ending it now. But I need information. I need to find them. It's not too late. It can't be. We're a team, and I'll do everything I can to save them.

Her spectacles…

With my free hand, I pluck them off her face and put them on my own nose. "Follow me," I say, grabbing her roughly by the arm as I keep the zapper trained on her. We head down the corridor, away from the lab, and hopefully ahead of the virus.

She glares at me as I press a button, trying to acclimate to the unfamiliar interface. It's obviously been programmed and made with her in mind, and her eyes must be closer together than mine, because the viewing angle is a little off for me. But if I squint and cross my eyes, I can see most of it.

And, to my utter pleasure, there's a map of Alpha within the memory of the device. As I sort my way through the information, using my eyes to direct the computer, I pull up a section of the station that says *Infirmary*, but the good doctor has left a note nicknaming it *The Dungeon*.

That makes me even more pissed.

There's a log of all the occupants in there. A child, a large female cyborg, a skinny male and a bigger male, both cyborgs as well. Definitely the crew of the *Pícara*, and they're on the complete opposite end of the station, like they were trying to separate us as much as possible.

There's also a warning flashing on the lens, alerting everyone that there's been an outbreak on the station. A simulation shows the spread of the virus as it accelerates the further it goes. Just like a nightmare, the more it infects, the faster it moves.

And with the crew on the opposite end, it's going to be a tight race. Dr. Jackson wasn't lying when she said that if the virus was out, then I wouldn't be able to get to them in time.

I'm at least going to try.

"Where's the android?" I ask as we move down the hall.

"What?"

"The navigation android," I say impatiently. "He's not listed among those in the infirmary. Where is he?"

Her nostrils flare in defiance. "*He* was dismantled just after your ship docked. He was unreasonable and inconsolable with the state he was in. And with the *Pícara* being a biohazard piece of junk, we saw fit to junk him as well."

No. It can't be. Orion can't be gone. My heart clenches inside my metal rib cage as the rage overtakes me, and I backhand her with the zapper, blood flying as she collapses to the ground. "Where are his parts?" I screech. "Tell me, or so help me…"

I trail my voice, meaning to be threatening, but she only gives a low laugh. "You think I'm the monster here?" she asks. "Me?" She glares up at me, her eyes shooting venom my way. "You're the one who made a deal with a virus to get your way."

Her words hit me just as hard as my blow to her. I take a shuddering breath as I look down at her, feeling something like pity and horror mixed together.

But then something akin to apathy settles on me. At some point during my containment, I've stopped caring about what it means to be good or bad. The only thing I can do is protect those I care about. And it's time for me to keep moving, to do whatever it takes to save them. Even at the cost of my humanity.

We both twist our heads to see the virus coming around the corner, a trail of liquid as red as blood. It's on the floor and on the walls, and it flows its way menacingly towards us.

It's time to move.

"I am what I have to be," I tell her, "because this is the world that you manufactured for me. I had no choice—I'm a victim of this thing that you created."

She only shakes her head at me. "You've killed everyone on the station," she says softly. "You've caused a larger, deadlier outbreak than what happened on Delta. We were trying to find an antivirus here. We were trying to suppress it."

I jangle the bag carrying the vials next to me. "So you could infect a population and then have them buy your week-long treatment?"

She doesn't deny it, and that almost makes it even worse. But before she says anything, her eyes shoot up towards the ceiling as the red goop starts to trickle down towards her. She doesn't move; she doesn't protest. She only stares at it, open-mouthed, as the virus infects her, making her a part of the bigger lifeform.

"And look what that brought you," I say hollowly before I take off sprinting along the route on the map. I don't feel any remorse for what happened to her.

I'm a cyborg hellbent on a mission now. And the stars won't be able to help anyone who gets in my way.

MY DAMAGED LEG doesn't hinder me too much as I sprint. My cyborg side makes up for my weakened biological side, so even though my muscles have atrophied, I can still make my way down the corridors. Emergency sirens are blaring, and residents—both androids and Lifers alike—pass me going the opposite direction, evacuating the station.

Despite everything, I hope they're able to escape the virus and prove Dr. Jackson wrong. I don't want to be responsible for their deaths, even if they were necessary for me to get out of captivity. Apparently, I still have a human heart.

Through one of the hallways, I reach an annex in what looks to be a downtown residential area of Alpha, a fully enclosed city within the spaceport. According to the spectacles, civilians live in the center while the administrative functions happen in a ring around it. Condominiums stretch along both sides of the street, so tightly packed I can't see the end of the street or what lays beyond these buildings. There's a sizable city spread out before me, a good twenty miles across, according to Dr. Jackson's spectacles.

And everyone is trying to leave it all at once. Delta's demise must have scared them to action, because they all look like they're about to meet their maker.

I can't believe how many Lifers live on Alpha. I've never seen so many humans with their bodies fully intact before. One of the hallmarks of a Free Agent is the presence of a bionic part—kind of like sharing stories about scars from old Earth. The more fortunate Lifers never had to worry about space debris, or their containment breaching and being sucked out into space.

They've all lived charmed lives. And now? It's their Armageddon.

People dash from all directions, stampeding each other and shouting for everything to get out of the way. I have to duck around them, going against the flow of panicked traffic.

I should have taken a different approach, but Dr. Jackson's spectacles are telling me this is the most direct route to The Dungeon, even with the traffic. I just have to keep going. At least that's what I keep telling myself.

"Watch it, you fucking cyborg!" someone snaps at me as I bump into him. He carries an armful of goods for his family of three. I make eye contact with a girl who can only be his daughter based on their shared ginger hair. She's only about six years old. Her eyes are so wide, there's more white than irises and pupils.

She's around the same age I was when Louis found me. And she may not get off this hunk of metal alive.

I turn to her father, even though he had cursed me out. They don't deserve to die, not at the hands of the virus.

"Go to the docks on the starboard side," I tell him, pointing in a direction that is a forty-seven-degree deviation from everyone else's path. The spectacles are telling me which areas of Alpha are flooded with evacuees, and there's far fewer at that dock than any other. "There are some escape pods there that have not been used yet, and it's far enough from the virus that you won't be at risk of infection."

He frowns at me, in disbelief at first, and then takes in my hospital gown outfit, the bag on my shoulder, and the zapper in my hand. "Why are you telling me this?" he asks.

"Because you need to save your daughter," I say, nodding to the girl who looks like she's about to pass out.

He doesn't budge. "How can I trust a cyborg like you?"

Did I mention that Lifers have a horrible prejudice against Free Agents? It pisses me off.

"Just go!" I say, giving him a rough push. He stumbles, dragging his daughter and wife along with him, giving me a suspicious glare as they continue walking. To my relief, they're moving in a different path than the rest of the crowds.

Maybe he's not an idiot and he'll save his family. Hopefully that will teach him not to look down upon cyborgs.

But I doubt it.

Another alarm blares, this time more insistent than the first one. The spectacles tell me that the virus has taken out an entire side of the ship, rendering it impassable due to the spreading infection. I also receive a notification that the Feds have been alerted and they'll be here in 25.7 minutes.

That's even less time than I had planned on initially.

"Fuck," I mutter under my breath as I look around for some sort of vehicle. There are still eighteen clicks between me and the Dungeons, and while I could have made it in my peak condition, I'm injured and weak. My only hope is to find something that will take me there.

Miraculously, I spot an air scooter that no one else has thought to take in their mad scramble out of the main city. I swing my leg over it and secure the bag before I transform my right index finger into a tool that will jumpstart the bike without a keycode. It's risky, and I can get electrocuted from the scooter, but it's a risk I'm willing to take.

"C'mon, c'mon, c'mon…"

The scooter roars to life, and I let out an excited whoop, which catches the attention of some evacuees.

"Hey!" one shouts. "Take me with you! Take me—!"

I hit the accelerator, and the air scooter shoots off into the air above them, at such a fast speed I don't hear their cries behind me. I didn't have the time to tell them that I'm going on a suicide mission. Even though I'm sure they would have knocked me off and used it themselves.

I am a cyborg, after all.

With the increased speed, my spectacles tell me that I'll make it to the Dungeons in a little over six minutes. That's a much better estimate than I had earlier, but I refuse to let myself celebrate just yet.

Hovering twenty feet above the crowds, I can see the sheer swell of bodies as they press toward every available exit. Other air vehicles fly by me, and I have to watch out for collisions.

But the miles fly by underneath me, and I make it to the end of the main city, toward the edge of the dome that makes up Space Port Alpha. As I park the scooter, I wonder if there's any way I can keep it—once I find the crew, I'll have to find Orion somewhere on this space port, and I may need it.

I decide against it in the end. Let someone else have a chance.

I push through the door and find myself in another hallway, this one less empty than the rest of the space port. Maybe everyone has evacuated the Dungeons, and the members of the crew have all been saved. I can hope, right?

But the spectacles say they're still there, captured.

Just a few more doors, and I spot the sign that says *Infirmary*.

"Or as Dr. Jackson calls it, the *Dungeon*," I mutter as I palm the touchpad next to the door. Nothing happens. Of course, it would be locked. If Taka were on this side of the door, he'd be able to access the code in thirty seconds flat. As it is, I'm not as good at that, but I can try.

I dismantle the screen and pull apart a few wires. My retina replays video of Taka doing this exact same thing, and I use it as an instruction manual for hacking this door myself. I mess up a few times, causing it to beep angrily at me, but then, finally, when I press two wires together, the doors iris open.

I nearly sob in relief at the open door, but my revelry is short-lived. As I step into the Dungeons, I see why Taka hasn't tried hacking the system himself.

All around me are cryogenic capsules, similar to the one they kept me in the lab, only these are meant for extended prison sentences, keeping the captives alive when the Feds decided that death wasn't a good enough punishment for the worst offenders. Why waste perfectly good specimens for experiments?

There are thousands here spiraling upwards around the edges of the Dungeon, making me wonder exactly what Dr. Jackson had in mind for testing. Especially since this was originally called The Infirmary. Did she mean to experiment on them later? Use them to spread the virus? Or create something entirely new?

As I look at them, I wonder if I had been in one of these capsules at one point in my life. I gnaw at my bottom lip, feeling that sense of dread clench my stomach.

Then the spectacles alert me that another ward in Alpha has fallen to infection, shortening the estimated time for the ship to fall victim to it. I can't stay here and wonder about what might have been.

Keep it together, Clem, I tell myself. I suck in a deep breath, trying to steady my rapidly beating heart. Just find them and get out. That's all I need to save them.

I break into another pad for access to the files and numbers of the captives—wasting precious time when there's a deadly virus headed our way. Luckily for me, everyone is grouped together, meaning that I just need to call that section of the prisoners. Huge, mechanical arms begin moving, going their respective direction to pull four different capsules that are placed in front of me.

A sigh of relief catches in my throat, and I wipe the frost off the capsule closest to me. PC's slumbering face greets me, and I almost thump the window to say hi. Not that it would work—they're all in deep sleeps right now, and if I have any hope of getting them out of here, I need to wake them up.

I turn the mechanical lock on the front, and it hisses open with a burst of cold air. Inside, I hear PC coughing.

He's alive. Thank the stars, he's alive!

I move to the other capsules, opening them up as quickly as possible, and they all hiss open to reveal the groggy, slumbering prisoners inside. Everyone seems fine. Everyone is in one piece.

"Cl—Clementine?" PC asks. I turn as he sits up in his capsule, a dark, skintight uniform flush against his body, leaving nothing to the imagination. I've seen him naked before, so it's no big deal, but these uniforms are one last insult to the prisoners.

"Hey, PC," I tell him.

"What are you doing here?" He blinks at me, frowning deeply. "Are you still infected? Where's Louis?"

The mention of our former captain hurts me almost physically, and I grimace as I look at him. He's not too drowsy to pick up on my distress, and his face hardens as he watches me. "What happened?" he asks, his voice steely.

"Not enough time to explain," I say as I press a button on the side of the spectacles so my human computer downloads all the information on the drive. Daisy, Taka, and Oliver sit up in their capsules, their attention on me. The perfect time to fill them in on everything. Hopefully they aren't too dazed to understand.

"It's a month later," I say. "We are on Space Port Alpha. And the virus is loose here, and if it doesn't get us first, the Feds will blow us up."

I don't tell them that I made a bargain with the virus to escape. That's something to share when we've had a few drinks.

Maybe. I still wonder if I'm a monster for selling myself out like that.

"Daisy," I say, taking off the spectacles. I hand them to her because she's the fastest runner of the bunch, and she gives them a quizzical look, not understanding what they are. "Take these and go towards the nearest docks. And I want you to commandeer a ship for us."

"A ship?" she asks, confused. "But what about the *Pícara*?"

Another blow to my fragile façade of being the brave leader. I try smiling encouragingly, but it fails. "It's infected, too," I say. "They have it as a biohazard, and I don't think it's safe to fly. Not unless you want to get infected."

"And you?" PC asks. "Are you infected?"

"That's…complicated," I say. "And we don't have time for it. What I need you to do is find a ship we can steal."

"And what about you?" Taka asks.

I swallow back the thrill of fear. "I need to go find Orion," I say. "They dismantled him somewhere, and I need to find what's left of him and bring him back. And if I'm not back in ten—"

"You're not doing that alone," PC says, grimacing as he gets to his feet. "I'm coming with you."

"You can barely stand, PC."

"And you're wearing a paper gown," he retorts back. "So you don't have a leg to stand on. Mechanical or otherwise."

His comment strikes me as a joke, and I start chuckling in hysterics, clutching at my hair. He grins, knowing that he has me wrapped around his finger.

"Fine," I say, holding up my hands, "but it's risky."

"And so was downlooting a dangerous virus," Daisy mutters, "but we can't stay away from trouble, can we?" She nods to Taka and Oliver. "We'll find you a ship, Clem. Just make sure you're back in time. Even if you can't find Orion. Androids are replaceable. You aren't."

I wanted to tell her that Orion is irreplaceable, too, but I don't have the time nor energy to fight her. Or explain that one. So I just nod. "Call us with the location of the ship," I say, tapping my temple. "And we'll be there in ten minutes."

"Right," Daisy says as she puts the spectacles on. She pulls herself out of the capsule and doesn't even sway on her feet as she gestures for the others to join her. "Taka, Oliver, let's move!"

The two males pull themselves out of their containers, although Oliver needs some help from Daisy. "Good luck, Clementine," the boy says as Daisy grabs his hand, and they start running.

I turn towards PC. "You know you're stupid for coming along with me."

He grins snidely at me. "You know I can't let you kill yourself over an android. Even if you're in love with him."

I open my mouth to make a retort, but that would just be another lie. So I let out an exasperated breath and walk towards the door, hoping that can be the end of that conversation.

"So where do you think they keep dismantled androids?" PC asks behind me. "Do you have any of that info from that thing you downloaded?"

"No," I say flatly. I hold up the zapper. "But I suggest we find someone who does."

A wicked smile comes to my surrogate brother's face. "I like the way you think."

Chapter 23

There's one thing that PC and I know going into this: trying to find a dismantled android on a space station during an evacuation is like trying to find a speck of space dust in an asteroid field. We both know that it's close to impossible, but to my relief, PC doesn't try to talk me out of it or say that we shouldn't keep looking.

The only obvious place I can think of is the junkyard, a place all space ports have where they recycle metal and computer components to sell or to repair the port itself. A lot of the Free Agent space stations are made up primarily of space junk, but this Lifer base is immaculate.

I wonder what kind of junkyard we'll find, because most junkyards I've been to have been piled high with tons of rubbish. If Orion is in there, we may never find him.

But we keep heading toward the location on the map my retina shows me.

PC and I move together in a unit, with me at the front wielding my zapper while he follows at my back, keeping an eye out for any looters. I keep the bag of vials close at hand. I thought I should give them to Oliver, but in case I don't make it in time, I need to have them with me for however long I'll live.

"So what happened to you?" PC asks, his tone oddly conversational.

"What do you mean?"

"Well, last time I saw you, you were unconscious on the floor after Venice touched you and turned into sewage." He grimaces at the memory. "Orion went *nuts* for you, you know. He immediately went to the bridge, and no matter what we tried telling him, he refused to go anywhere but Alpha. You were infected, you know. We all thought you were going to die."

It feels odd, hearing this story now after a month of speculating what happened. "And then?" I ask.

He frowns. "Well, we docked, and everything seemed peachy keen until the doors opened and the soldiers came in wearing biohazard suits. They knew exactly what they were getting into, Clem. They were treating this like some sort of recovery operation."

"It was," I mutter, remembering how happy Maas was that he found one of the virus's original test subjects. "They told me that they had to power down Orion before they were able to retrieve me," I add quietly.

"They shot him with a zapper first—with a blast that was meant to kill, and if he'd been a human, he'd be dead."

No wonder they used him for scraps. I grit my teeth. "They're assholes," I say.

PC snorts derisively. "That's the understatement of the century. Then they fired at us, and...the next thing I know, you're waking me up in that glorified casket."

I nod. "Basically, that's it."

"But...what happened to you, Clem?"

"I was infected," I say, "and now I have it under control."

PC stops short and gives me a hard look. "You mean you're—"

I shrug, not wanting to get into it. And footsteps save me from having to explain further. Both PC and I fall silent as we sidle up to a wall to see our intruder coming around the corner. I meet PC's eyes as we both wait…

And then I step out in front of the human running along the hallway. He's a civilian, with a bandana tied around his forehead, with the distinct grease stains and look of a mechanic. In fact, he looks like a less severe version of Daisy.

As luck would have it, we've found one of the very people who may know where Orion is. I remember Maas wondering if there was a higher power that controlled everything. I'm starting to wonder that myself.

Without a cyborg part to help regulate his vitals, he immediately starts hyperventilating as he stares down the barrel of my firearms.

I level the zapper at him. "Quiet, or I'll kill you," I say. PC gives me a surprised look, but I'm not playing games. Time is running out, and we have to get going.

"Please don't kill me," the man says, and I smell ammonia. The poor man's pissed himself, he's so frightened at being held at gunpoint. I almost feel bad.

"Are you a mechanic here on Alpha?" I ask.

He swallows, the knob in his throat bobbing up and down. "For ten years, ma'am."

"So you're familiar with the junkyard then?"

He hesitates, his eyes flicking to PC, as if begging for help.

"Answer me," I growl.

"Somewhat?" the man says, sounding unsure.

Maybe we don't have a miracle here. I fight back the disappointment that tries to bubble out of my throat. "I have an android that I'm looking for that has been wrongly dismantled. Where would you keep him?"

He blinks. "What?"

I cock the zapper. "Android. Dismantled. Where?"

The man glances back at PC again, his expression confused. "Hey, don't look at me," PC says with a shrug. "The lady's asking you a question, I suggest you answer."

"We'd, uh, put the android in the junkyard," the man says.

I don't move my gun. "Take me to it. And the faster you do that, the faster I'll let you go."

The man nods wildly, looking between us. "Okay, okay, okay!"

He scrambles back in the direction he came, and I see the reason why he's acting shifty. He has a pack full of parts that he must have looted. Some of the electronics are brand new, making his haul impressive.

I don't really care as we follow him back out to the main dome, and he ducks into a silo that hugs the side of the dome. My inner map tells me that this is the largest of the three junkyards on the station.

There's two others. And I can't help the rising panic if we are going to the wrong one.

The man palms open the door, meaning that he's actually far more familiar with junkyards than he had originally let on. The door opens, and the three of us step inside.

Remarkably, despite the evacuation, the junkyard remains untouched, even though looting is rampant in the main city. It's either a sign that the residents know there's nothing here worth looting or they're already so well off, they don't care about a load of junk.

It's mostly a pile of different metals, wires, pieces of glass, and even some other trash that the residents of the stations have discarded. The pile is nearly thirty feet tall and feels remarkably unstable as I peer up at it.

"We usually keep them here," the man says, gesturing for

us to follow him. He rounds the base of the pile toward the other side, and…

"Orion," I breathe, almost in disbelief. My zapper on the man wavers as I look at what remains of the android, piled on top of other broken and discarded androids, like a mass grave.

True to what I'd been told, he's been dismantled. His arms and legs are gone, leaving him as a quadruple amputee. Thankfully, though, his torso is mostly intact, which is where his personality is housed. We can find replacements for his arms and legs. We can't find a replacement for *him*.

"PC, can you see if you can find some arms and legs for him?" I ask. "Just…anything to tide him over until we can find replacements." Surely in this pile of stuff, we can find something for him.

"Uhhh, sure," PC says as he jogs over and starts digging through it.

The man clears his throat, drawing my attention back over to him. "You're free to go," I say, gesturing with the zapper. As the man turns, I shout, "Wait!"

The man freezes midstride, as if expecting me to shoot him in the back. That's not what I had in mind, though. I grab a spare arm out of his pack that he must have picked up when he looted the city. "I've got a left arm," I shout to PC as I take it with me. The man gapes at me, and I gesture for him to keep going.

He runs.

Now to get Orion.

I tug him out of the pile, trying to ignore his naked body—which is generously anatomically correct—and gently lean him against the wall. I crouch in front of what remains of the android and get the uneasy feeling that he's dead. There's something so strange about a part of a body that's so still, especially when it's someone I care about.

Will he boot up? I guess there's only one way to find out.

I reach for his right ear lobe, where there's an on-switch, and flip it on.

Three agonizing seconds pass by as I wait, wondering if he's damaged beyond all repair.

Suddenly, a light flickers behind those familiar eyes, and he blinks slowly. "Clementine?" He sounds disoriented, as he should be since he just woke up in a strange new place without his limbs and facing the person who he thought had died.

"Hey," I say, smiling at him. "I heard you got into some trouble."

"You are alive?" he asks, relief in his voice.

I nod. "You saved everyone by bringing us to Alpha."

He tries to move, but he quickly finds that he's limited in movement, so he just blinks rapidly and makes a pained face. "Why can I not move?"

"That's because," PC says, jumping down from a spot on the pile, carrying two legs and a mismatched arm, "you were blasted by some zappers the second we landed on Alpha. You went crazy back there."

Orion watches him for a confused moment before turning his attention back on me. "I did," he admits, almost musing to himself. "I did lose myself back there. And are you okay, Clementine?"

I snicker softly. "Well, we're here and alive. But not for much longer if we don't move. PC, can you carry him somehow?" I realize then that I had no idea how I'd get him to the ship without PC's help.

He sometimes knows best.

"Always making me do the hard work," he grumbles good-naturedly.

I roll my eyes as I check how long we have. 157.7 seconds until I told Daisy and the others to leave us due to the infection spreading that much closer. And who knows if they actually made it to the docks and found a ship.

As if reading my thoughts, I'm alerted to an incoming call, and I immediately answer it. "Where are you?" Taka asks on the other line. "We have a ship, but for not much longer. I'll send you the coordinates."

A second later, a blip appears on my retina map, showing their location. We can make it before the virus gets to them if we sprint. I glance over to see what PC has done with Orion and nearly laugh out loud. He has the android in a sling with the spare parts sticking out at odd angles. Orion doesn't look too happy at the arrangement, but at least they're both ready, too.

"We'll be there," I promise Taka as I turn off the call. "PC, follow me."

And we break into a run.

Chapter 24

There's an unspoken desperation between the three of us as PC and I sprint even faster than before. The deadline is too close for us to make light of the situation. All we can do is run.

I can't help but feel like our luck will run out and we won't make it to the ship in time. Either the infection will catch up to us or we'll be caught or Daisy will be forced to leave without us.

We don't speak to each other as we move, not even bothering to try to move stealthily—the hallways and the main city are mostly empty by this point, and the only things we have to dodge now are scattered signposts, trashcans, and broken glass.

My retina counts down the timer, a constant reminder that time is running out until the virus reaches us. I can't see the virus, but I feel it behind us, reaching out towards me.

I exchange an uneasy glance with PC as I pass him, and the dock comes into sight.

We're so close. So damn close. Just a little further and we can leave this nightmare behind. At least for now until I have to figure out another solution for my infection.

A blast from a zapper goes wide and fries the doorframe in

front of us. Both PC and I screech to a halt, freezing as there's someone who's armed behind us. I meet PC's gaze, and his eyes glance behind me, going wide.

"Miss Jones." I cringe at the voice behind me. How could he have found me in the pandemonium during the outbreak? And now of all times, when we're so damn close to making it off this doomed station.

I slowly turn around and see Chairman Maas standing behind me with a group of soldiers poised in front of him, their zappers aimed directly at us. The message is clear: the first shot was a warning, the next will be to kill.

For a 140-year-old man, Maas looks rather spry as he crosses his arms, looking at us. "There is one ship left in the dock with an intrepid crew keeping everyone from boarding it. Everyone but you and your companions here."

"We stole it fair and square," PC says.

Maas pointedly ignores him. "I thought you were destined for great things, Miss Jones. I just never thought you'd be the cause of an outbreak like this."

PC glances at me. "What?"

I open my mouth to protest, but what am I supposed to do? I give him a helpless expression, but he looks at me like I'm some sort of alien. Over his shoulder, Orion watches me calmly, as if he's trying to see if this is fake or not.

Maas titters in laughter. "Oh, you didn't tell your crew how you escaped?"

"PC, he's just trying to keep us from getting to the ship," I say softly. "There was never a cure for Louis. There was never a 300 million Space Yen payout. What he wanted to do was have us deliver him a virus so that he could take over the galaxy and monetize treatment for it."

"Such brave words from a young woman," Maas says, "who is still infected with the virus."

Both PC's and Orion's eyes widen. "What?" they ask together.

"I have it under control," I tell them.

"And I thought I had it under control as well," Maas says, spreading his hands wide. "And look at what it did to my space station. All because this wench is unpredictable. She'll kill you just to get her way."

"You know that's not true," I whisper, closing my eyes.

"I can't let her off this space station," Maas says. "She'll infect the rest of the galaxy. She'll do exactly what you've been trying to avoid."

I look at PC, pleading with my eyes to believe me. Believe me about what, I'm not sure, as everything Maas says has either been true or can be a possibility. But this is his game; this is what he wants.

We can't just give it to him.

PC watches me and gives the barest of nods. Relief spreads throughout my body that despite everything, my adoptive brother still trusts me. When the world goes to hell, I can trust my family and friends.

Now is just the waiting game. Because as we stand there, my timer counts down to zero, heralding the arrival of the virus in our section. My stomach clenches in warning, sensing it coming ever so closer. I welcome the distraction but hate coming face to face with it again.

Some things are unavoidable, though. And if I have to face the virus again to save everyone, I will.

"What do you have to say for yourself, Miss Jones?" Maas taunts. I hear the clicks of the zappers as the soldiers ready themselves to shoot at me, like a firing squad. I wish I could say that I feel nervous about that, but after everything that has happened, I am just out of fucks to give.

So I lay it on the line for him and everyone present.

"What do I have to say?" I ask through gritted teeth. "You

dare ask me that? When you paid desperate parents for their children just so you could experiment on them? And you've spent the last twenty-five years trying to develop a virus worse than the space flu, just so you can wipe out the competition? When you're willing to do everything to make a buck? Am I painting a good picture for you yet?"

I see the zappers waver the longer I speak. The chairman may feel 100% confident in his troops' loyalty, but it's hard to believe that's true when the head of your company is willing to lay your life on the line.

"It's just business," Maas says coldly, narrowing his eyes at me. "Any other corporation with our resources would have taken the same chances."

"And the fall of Delta is just business, too?" I put my hands on my hips. "Hundreds of thousands of people dying from a virus you can't control?"

More wavering. I'm getting through to the soldiers.

"Delta was not our fault," Maas says coldly. "I told you that there was a rogue scientist who tried selling our secrets to the competition."

"Because of practices like this. All you corporations are the same."

Some of the zappers finally lower as the soldiers stand up straighter, my words finally hitting home with them.

But by this point, it's too late for them. I gnaw on my bottom lip as I see the wave of crimson rounding the corner. I can almost feel the pull of the virus, calling out to me, inviting me to join it in its quest for domination.

"And you all can go fuck yourselves," I mutter at the group.

I hold my ground as the wave of the virus sweeps through the group of soldiers, bowling over Maas, and the old man lands on top of the soldiers. The screams just as loud as I remember Louis's scream was, and I wince as I step away. PC does the same thing out of reflex, trying to put as much distance between him and the virus.

"We have to go!" he shouts above the din, grabbing at my arm.

I nod dazedly. "Yes," I agree. I can no longer see Maas as a separate entity among the surge of the virus, although I see one of those clear blue eyes watching us. "Long live the chairman," I say to it. "And fuck you."

We have to leave now. PC palms the door, and it easily opens, showing us the dock. And as we step through the door, we both slow, seeing Taka sit in front of a huge cruiser space ship complete with torpedo bays and an awesome paint trim on the side.

The engineer smiles at us and gets to his feet, hefting his own zapper in his hands. He takes off the spectacles and crunches them under his feet as a final farewell to Alpha. "Didn't think you guys would make it," he says.

"We got caught up," I say as we run up the ramp. PC glances at me, his expression suspicious, but he doesn't mention what Maas said. I could hug him for that. "We need to move. *Now*."

"Daisy has it all fired up," Taka says, ushering us onto the platform, leading up to the ship. "We just needed you guys." He tilts his head towards Orion. "Glad to see you again," he adds amusedly.

"I have been better," Orion says with a smirk.

"Thank you for waiting," I say softly. "Thank you so damn much."

"Of course," Taka says, "you're our captain."

I slow, hearing his words. This entire time, I've been thinking in terms of Louis getting better and taking the title of captain again. But I know for certain that he will never fly again. I look out towards the dock as the loading ramp closes behind us, giving me one last glimpse of Louis's, Venice's, and the *Pícara's* final resting place. So many memories and good times, all wash away because of a stupid mistake.

I don't know if I'm fit to be captain. I sigh and grab one of the side seats, putting my bag in my lap and holding it to me like it's everything precious I have in life as the ship jolts from the initial liftoff. I don't have a window to the outside world right now, which is probably a good thing. I don't want to see the space station that I doomed to a certain death.

I close my eyes and lean back against the cold metal of the bay, calming myself. My retina is telling me all my vitals, reminding me that I'm still alive. Like everyone else on board.

With Orion in his lap, PC eyes me warily. "You're going to have to talk to me about what happened back there," he says in a low voice. "About what Maas said."

I glance at him and give a sad smile. "Someday," I say. "Just not now."

PC watches me for a long moment before nodding. "Okay," he says. "Okay."

Orion watches me as well, and I'm glad that he doesn't add anything to what PC said. I don't think I can handle both their scrutiny at the moment. Not after everything that happened.

I feel the ship lurch as it hits FTL, blasting away from the crippled space station. The Feds will arrive and then destroy the virus.

I almost feel bad for it.

I stiffen as I hear, *Be seeing you, Clementine*. And I wonder if I had imagined that myself or if the virus is communicating through my mind somehow.

I ignore it and settle back on my seat and close my eyes.

"Captain," Daisy says on the intercom, "where would you like to go?"

Without opening my eyes, I murmur softly, "Anywhere but here."

Chapter 25

"There we go," Daisy says, sitting back from her handiwork. She wipes her hands with a proud smile on her face. "That ought to do it."

Before her, Orion looks down at his new hands and wiggles the toes of his feet. Daisy has spent the last two days putting the cyborg back together again with Taka's help. Between the two of them, they fashioned something resembling a human, even if his hands are different sizes and colors and one leg is shorter than the other. It's a far cry from where Orion had been.

"Thank you," he says softly. "I never would have thought that I would miss my limbs so much."

"That's because you don't like being dependent on anyone else," I say crossing my arms. "But in this case, you needed us."

"Yeah, especially since he doesn't like accepting any form of help," PC mutters. "Androids are as stubborn as female captains."

I can't hide my smile.

It's been a few days since leaving Alpha. Three days of

relaxing and trying to figure out what to do next, as there are too many details and questions ahead of us. But after everything that happened, we're taking this time to regroup and gather strength. After all, we lost a month of our lives on that space station—the universe can afford for us to take a little bit longer of a break.

I notice my timer near zero again, the important one that's keeping me from infecting everyone on this ship. I offer up a brave smile and get to my feet. "Well," I say, slapping my hands to my knees, "I'm going to go to bed."

PC blinks at me. "What?" he asks. "And miss out on poker?" Ever since we got onto this new ship—it's called the *Argo*—he hasn't approached me about explaining what Maas had told us before we docked. Both he and Orion have been very respectful in that case.

I'll have to tell them someday. But I don't want to face those demons of mine yet.

I shrug. "I'm just tired." I give a lazy wave. "See you tomorrow."

I get to my feet and make my way to my room. The captain's quarters are so unlike the quarters of the *Pícara*. It's more luxurious, for one. And it's much larger. I stand in the threshold, taking it all in. There's a vertical garden on one wall, growing herbs and succulents. The light is brighter, too, and less blue. I never realized how depressing our rooms were until I compared them to this one.

And this is our new ship. At least for now. Who knows how long we'll have it—we're fugitives.

But I can't help thinking that Louis would have loved it.

I push aside the thought of the former captain. I'm still grieving for him. And I know that I will continue to do so for some time. But I can't do it now. Not after everything I've done.

You're a monster.

I'm not human. Not machine, or even cyborg. *Monster.*

I walk over to the bed, running the fingers of my left hand over the walls, feeling the texture of it, how it's so different than the cold, steel walls of my childhood home. I pull out the backpack of vials from its hiding place underneath the bed and check the timer.

I cut it a little close this time.

I take one out and a syringe and measure the right amount and stick it into the fleshy part of my left shoulder. It burns as I press the plunger, but I don't have any bad side effects, at least not yet. It's uncomfortable, but it'll keep the Infinity Virus under control for now.

Stay dormant, I silently tell the virus. There's no answering call back, meaning that I've at least put enough of a leash on it to keep it quiet.

I should probably keep a vial with me at all times. In case I'm away from my room and can't get back in time. So many things to think about and to make sure that I don't cause another outbreak. I'm dangerous. I know it.

Funny how I don't feel any different.

There's a buzz at the door. I stash the vials before calling out, "Come in."

The door slides open, and my breath catches in my throat. "Orion."

For once, he looks nervous. There's an energy about him that I've never seen before. Like he's unsure of himself, which is something I don't think I've ever seen on the android before.

But I put on a smile. "Glad to see you walking around again."

He scratches behind his head. "Yes. You do not realize how much you miss it until you do not have it."

I nod. "I know."

"I have two items to talk to you about."

I nod. "Okay."

"First." He reaches behind his head, and, as he turns his head, I see a panel I've never noticed before in his hairline by his temple. Orion is full of surprises sometimes. He takes out a storage chip and holds it aloft. "This is a backup of all the systems of the *Pícara*. I downloaded them before we arrived on Alpha. In case we never saw the ship again." He gives me a smile. "I have only now been able to access it since I have hands."

I blink a few times, trying to understand what he means. "You mean…you have everything from the *Pícara* there?"

He nods. "Videos, travel logs, captain's diaries, and certain *idiosyncrasies*." He smiles about that last part, showing me that he knew the ship had a personality. "They are all here. I know how much the ship meant to you and Popcorn. So here it is."

I take it from him, and I can't help my own grin that spreads across my face. "How was it having the *Pícara* in your systems?" I ask. "She never really did like me."

He gives a nonchalant shrug. "The *Pícara* was an old ship that had picked up many bad habits in its time. If I could preserve it, I wanted to do so."

I clutch it to my chest, feeling a sense of relief that I hadn't lost everything with the metal ship. I can't believe that I'm about to voluntarily bring that ship's personality back on this perfectly fine ship. I think about the cold showers I'll have in the future, the doors randomly closing on me, things not working…

And I'm excited to have it back.

"Thank you," I whisper. "Thank you so much."

"There is another thing," Orion says, and his expression hardens. "I want you to erase an event from my memory banks."

My euphoria from knowing that the *Pícara* will be back fades. I look up at him, confused. Hurt. "What event?"

"The kiss."

Oh. My mouth opens for a retort, I can't do that. I can't take the risk that I'll accidentally erase something else or change his behavior based on that one exchange. *No.* No, I can't do it. I don't want to go back to before. I don't want to remember the kiss while he doesn't.

"I'm so sorry that happened," I say. "I was grieving, and—"

"It...*changed* something in me, Clementine," Orion says, and my heart shudders to a halt. "When I thought you had been infected and were dying, I acted out of my feelings for you, not for the good of the crew or the ship. I put the crew at risk for one person. And..." The hard lines of his face fade away, and he looks unsure once again. "I cannot have that impacting my decisions."

"But...it happened," I say. "And just because you want it erased, it doesn't mean it goes away. I'll still remember it."

He nods. "And I apologize for that. But I cannot have it impacting my performance. I cannot have it drive me in illogical ways."

Illogical. That's what he thinks of this. My buried feelings for him. The way he thinks of me. He thinks it's illogical. And it probably is.

But we can't just pretend that it didn't happen. I don't know if I can.

"Please?" he asks. "I want to be the navigator I was programmed to be. And I think omitting that event will reset any inconsistencies."

And my resolve weakens. If that's what he wants...

I close my eyes. "Okay. Okay, fine. I'll do it. If you trust me not to mess you up." I hold my cyborg hand out and call my fingers to turn into the tools I need to access the memory banks in his brain. I'll have to connect to him and sift around through his memories in order to delete that instance.

And hopefully not fuck it up.

Relief spreads across his face. "I do trust you. Thank you, Clementine."

He takes a spot on the edge of my bed, his back to me, ready for the procedure. I can't help but think that I'd been wanting him on my bed for different reasons.

But that's apparently not going to happen now.

I hesitate for just a moment before I sweep aside his thick dark hair and access his core at the base of his neck. I hold back the shakes in my fingers as I work. Orion is eerily still as I work, and I use it to remind myself that he is not human.

He is an android. And I must remember that.

Even if his lips were the softest I'd ever kissed. Even if I'll never taste him again. This will be the most intimate I'll ever get with him—digging through his memories. I try to avoid any that feel too…personal to him. Which is ridiculous since he is a machine.

But I don't want to see anything I don't like. So I keep searching.

"Sometimes, I do reflect on whether events had unfolded differently," he says suddenly.

I lick my lips. "How do you mean?"

"If I had been a human instead of a machine. Maybe I would not be bound by protocol to put the crew and the ship above everything else." He pauses. "Maybe it would have been all right to remember that kiss."

I grit my teeth as I find the singular event. "We'll never know, will we?"

And I delete the kiss from his memory. Forever.

The Rogue's Galaxy

"ARE you sure you want to bring the *Picara* back?" PC asks. "I thought you had a supposed feud with the ship."

"It's what Captain Louis would have wanted," I answer.

We all watch as Taka works on the central console of the ship's bridge. Like everything else on this ship, it's far fancier than the *Picara's*. There are more cameras across the ship, better navigational maps.

And the view from the bridge is stunning. A complete 360-degree panorama of the galaxy as we sail through it—I feel like I can just extend my hand and capture a star.

Daisy, PC, Orion, and Oliver sit in chairs that they've chosen, although there are enough here to sit twenty. Maybe we'll fill them with more pirates coming up. Surely there are more people who want to overthrow the chokehold that these corporations have on the galaxy.

Wherever we go from here, I'll be glad to have my crew with me. We'll figure this out. We'll do it together.

I try to maintain my composure around Orion, who looks at me like I'm a complete stranger. No, scratch that—he looks at me like he knows me, but it's cold, distant. He's not the android I kissed.

And he won't ever remember it.

"All right, the chip is installed," Taka says as he gets to his feet from his crouch. "A reboot and that should do it." He wipes his hands.

"A reboot, huh? And that should be it?"

He nods. "If that is the full backup, it should assimilate with the current operating system and be able to control all the functions of the ship."

"Good job," I say appreciatively. "Thank you."

I key in the code for the ship's systems to restart. It won't bring back Louis or Venice. And it won't make this new ship the ship of my childhood.

But maybe I can bring a piece of my past with me into the future.

I initiate the restarting sequence.

The entire bridge goes dark, and the backup lights flicker off, for just a moment. I hold my breath, wondering what we're going to find when the ship is back online.

Unlike the *Pícara*, it boots up in seconds.

The lights turn on again, and the air system picks up and starts humming again. I glance around and feel a wide grin spread across my face.

"Did it work?" Daisy asks.

I look down at the console, and there's a message there. It's not much, and it doesn't say that I'll be battling the ship every morning.

But what I see is encouraging.

Welcome to the Pícara II, the screen says. I enlarge it on the window screen so that everyone else can see.

"I think it did." My grin widens. "Everyone, welcome to the *Pícara II*."

I'm almost ready to cry, and I can see Daisy sniffling as she looks at it. Even PC looks emotional. We have our ship back, sort of.

"Where to first, Captain?" Taka says, glancing back at me.

"Well," I say, slowly, looking at each member of the crew, memorizing their faces in this moment. I avert my eyes a little quickly from Orion. It's going to take some effort to hide my feelings for him. "We have a lot to do if we want to make some changes. Not to mention that Syn-Tech and possibly the Feds are looking for us. But," I look directly at Oliver, "we need to make a pitstop and pick up a robot pup for you."

His eyes widen as Daisy's stern face breaks into a wide grin.

"Really?" the boy asks, his voice quiet.

I nod. "Absolutely. This ship needs to have a puppy running around pissing oil in all the corners."

I feel a groan throughout the ship in response, like the *Picara II* is dreading the thought of that. She's back. And I can see it reflected on everyone's face.

My crew. My family.

And we're going to make our futures better for everyone.

To be continued in Book Two of The Infinity Project: *The Rogue's Paradox*, available for preorder now!

PREORDER NOW

Read on for a sneak peek...

I JUST STEPPED in robot dog piss.

It's not exactly piss—thankfully—but it's still black, oily, and gets all over my boots. I curse under my breath, lifting my foot up to see the oil dripping from the sole of my shoe.

It smells horrible. And it's the third time in as many days that I've stepped in oil slicks.

"Oliver!" I roar, twisting my head. "Oliver Twist!"

I hate playing the bad guy. I really do. But this is the exact reason why Captain Louis didn't want Oliver to have a robot pup on the old *Picara*, and now that we're on the *Picara II*, I especially don't want the little mongrel marking his territory on my brand-new ship.

And it's *my* ship because I'm the captain now. Which means that I need to enforce the rules.

The cabin boy comes running down the hallway, his mechanical pup trailing behind him, barking happily. Until it sees me, and then it cowers behind Oliver, whining with a high-pitched whir. For a nine-year-old boy, Oliver stands his ground, knowing that he's in trouble.

I admire that in him, so I have to hide my smile as I cross my arms.

"Wilbur's been marking his territory," I tell him, gesturing to my foot. "*Again*."

I watch as Oliver gulps nervously, then glances down at Wilbur, who growls at my mention of his name. "He doesn't mean to, Clem," Oliver says, "it's just his programming, and—"

"He's your responsibility," I say shortly. "You need to discipline him when he does this. You need to keep an eye on him."

I could very well be talking about myself at this point. The *Pícara II* and the crew are my responsibility. And I need to discipline them in order to keep a tight ship. And I feel like I'm failing them at every turn.

"But—" Oliver protests.

All it takes to shut him up is a raised eyebrow, and he stops. And I feel my heart clench at his wide eyes, remembering my own youth. Wilbur growls at me, sensing its owner's trepidation. I shoot my gaze towards the robot pup, and it quiets immediately.

For having messed up programming about marking territory, the dog is smart enough to know when not to push my buttons.

I decide that I've put enough fear in both of them, and I rub at my temples. "Just please, please, *please*, Oliver, keep an eye on Wilbur. I need you to do that for me."

I don't threaten to get rid of the robot, because I could never do that to the boy. But our hallways were so much cleaner before we got Wilbur. I know that the *Pícara II* herself doesn't appreciate it.

She's always had a bone to pick with me.

Oliver nods vigorously. "I will, Clem. I will!"

I allow myself to give him a small smile. "Good. Now get going. I know you probably have some chores that need to get done."

Oliver doesn't need to be told twice. "Thanks, Clem!" He takes off at a run, streaking past me, Wilbur nipping at his heels.

"And it should be *Captain* Clem to you!" I shout after him, although I can't stop sounding amused. I probably don't make as good a captain as Louis did, but I'm trying.

Galaxies know I'm trying.

"It's really not his fault," a voice says behind me. I turn my head to see my surrogate brother step out from behind the corner. PC smirks at me and nods towards Oliver's retreating back. "Taka's been working on Wilbur's programming to make him stop pissing all over the place."

"I know," I sigh. "But…"

"Hey," PC says, giving my shoulder a squeeze. "You're doing great."

I let out a whoosh of breath, slumping forward. That he knows me so well to see how much this whole thing has been wearing on me—it means a lot. I've seen myself in the mirror, the dark bags underneath my eyes that never seem to go away, the frown lines around my mouth that weren't there two months ago.

Those two months, and the few days that preceded them, have been the hardest in my life.

"It's so damn hard, PC," I murmur softly. "So damn hard."

"I know. It's going to be all right."

Is it? We're wanted fugitives, on the run from the Feds, with dwindling resources and money, and an uncertain future. Not to mention what I had to do to get to this point.

What I'm *still* doing to survive. My dirty secret that no one knows about. If PC knew what still runs through my veins and wires, he'd probably run scared.

Hell, I'm afraid of myself.

"Do you believe in life after death?" I murmur softly.

PC knows exactly what I mean by my question. "Not sure," he says finally with a shrug. "But if there is, I'm sure he'd be proud of you."

He being Captain Louis.

I close my eyes. He doesn't have to give me platitudes, PC knows that. He also knows that I hate bullshit. But I appreciate it. I need it, right now.

My retina computer gives me an alert. "Looks like dinner is ready," I say, opening my eyes. "Better not keep Daisy waiting."

If there's one thing that's scarier than her cooking, it's Daisy herself.

PC blanches, knowing exactly what that means. "I'd rather eat Wilbur's shit," he mutters.

Me too, even though I don't say it.

We head toward the mess hall, where Taka comes from the opposite end of the hallway, looking like he wants to do anything other than go inside.

"Hey, Taka." I give the engineer a smile. "Are you prepared for this?"

"No," he says simply with a shake of his head. "No, I am not. I'm still not recovered from lunch."

"I heard that!" The three of us jump at Daisy's thundering voice. The big woman appears in the doorway, an apron looking ridiculously tiny over her big bosom and waist. She holds a spatula in one hand, an oven mitt on the other, and there's some sort of slop smeared across her forehead. "You try making anything remotely edible with what we've got left."

Taka exchanges a nervous glance with PC, but I smile and push my way around Daisy. "We appreciate it, Daisy," I say empathically. After all, she's a mechanic, not a cook, so this is outside of her expertise. Granted, with a ship as big as the *Pícara II*, we're all taking on roles we're not familiar with.

Daisy just drew the short straw when it comes to cooking. And, unfortunately for all of us, she's not very good at it.

Then again, I never learned how to cook either, so I doubt I could do much better. So I can't complain. Not really.

Right?

But the smell hits me as I enter the room, and my stomach turns over unhappily. I wonder if I should try assigning someone else to kitchen duties, but PC tried his hand at a meal, and it was even more disastrous than this.

Taka wouldn't be much better.

The table is set with a few bowls filled with varying shades of gray slop. Daisy had unceremoniously stuck a spoon straight up in each one, and there's a pile of tin plates ready for us to eat off of.

I have to remind myself that I have to eat 2135 calories a day to maintain my weight, and I've already lost too much weight after the events on Alpha. A side effect of my many nightmares. My retina tells me that I have to make up for not eating during lunch, which means I'll have to have at least three helpings of the slop.

I hate to say it, but I would almost rather starve.

"Looks good," PC says behind me, his voice dripping with sarcasm.

"Now I know why Venice hated you lot," Daisy growls as she takes a seat. "No respect for how fucking hard this is."

"He didn't hate us," PC protests as he sits down as well. He sounds genuinely hurt by Daisy's words. "He was just lovably grumpy. All the time."

To be honest, I'm not sure which is true. Venice was always grousing about something, but we were assholes to him about his cooking. Now, I'd do anything to have him back.

I smile hollowly as I sit at the head of the table—where Captain Louis used to sit. Everything still feels surreal to me, like I'm living someone else's life. A lie. A lie that everything will be okay.

Taka's cheek twitches as he sits down. The color hasn't returned to his face, and he looks like he just ate a mouthful of space dust. Daisy glares at him, and he shies away from her stern expression.

"Are ya gonna eat?" Daisy asks.

"Not until the captain serves herself first," Taka answers quickly, looking my way.

Thanks a lot, asshole, I want to say to him as I summon the willpower to reach across the table and pick up the closest bowl. I spoon a heap onto a plate. "Is this chicken?" I ask, passing it to PC, who takes it with a barely disguised gag.

"That one's the veggies," Daisy says, ladling something else onto her own plate. "This one's the processed chicken. I think."

Not that any of us could tell the difference.

"Oh, ew," Oliver says from the door. He stands there with his eyes wide, and I wonder—not for the first time—if we need to figure out something different for a growing boy. Surely eating something disgusting like this every day isn't good for him.

Wilbur growls behind him.

"I really regret suggesting that damn dog," Daisy sighs, sitting back.

"What, why?" Oliver asks as he comes to the table. He takes a plate and puts a spoonful of *something* on it, and the dog's growl grows even louder.

Dairy frowns at the robot pup. "I thought they were supposed to be man's best friend or something?"

"Well, you'd have to be a man for that," Taka says absently, and she shoots him a glare. "What?"

She lets out an annoyed groan.

"It is times like these that make me glad I am not required to eat," another voice says mildly, and my heart skips a beat as I look up to see our navigator, Orion, standing behind Oliver. As an android, Orion matches the very definition of tall, dark, and handsome.

I press my lips together, trying to quell the remembered sensation of his mouth against mine. According to him, it never happened.

Yeah, right.

"Something tells me that we should be able to download a program to your system that makes you cook," Daisy says. "Taka?"

"That would require hooking up to the Net for far too long," the engineer says.

"Which is a definite *no*," I state in a flat voice. "We can't risk having someone trace the connection back to us."

"But PC is hooked up to the Net even now!" Daisy says, pointing to him.

PC looks up from his mini-tab, blinking at her accusation. "So?"

Her eyes boggle.

I clasp my hands in my front of me with a sigh. "PC's viewing the news on a secure connection, which is a different server than the android torrent servers." I give her a pointed look. "We're wanted people, Daisy, and they know that we'd be getting desperate. They know that we'd try to get more programs for our hardware."

"But the news—" Daisy protests.

"Is a calculated risk," I say softly, reminding myself of Captain Louis yet again. How many arguments did he dispel with a quiet voice and calm wisdom? I miss him with every fiber and wire of my being. "We have to know what's happening in the wider galaxy, otherwise we're sitting ducks."

"Speaking of what's happening out there," PC says, tapping on the screen of his mini-tab and it transfers to a hologram that pops up in the middle of the table. I grimace as I see an image of my face in front of me. The photo shows me with sallow cheeks and ashen skin, my hair wet and my eyes glassy. I've seen the picture before—it must have been taken while I was being held in captivity by Syn-Tech while they did tests on me.

"They increased your bounty, Clem," PC says. "One hundred billion Space Yen."

I stare at the number that says the same thing. *Clementine Jones. Wanted Dead or Alive for the Mass Genocide of Syn-Tech Alpha. Considered Armed and Dangerous. Reward: 1,000,000,000 SY.*

It's an impossibly high number. One that makes even me consider turning myself in. My entire crew would be set for life.

Daisy snorts. "Why not just offer up a bajillion gajillion Space Yen? It's all play money at that point."

"We're wanted, too," PC adds, tapping his screen again. The hologram shifts and it shows the entire crew's photos, even Oliver Twist, who had nothing to do with the events on Alpha. They all didn't have anything to do with what happened in Alpha.

I'm the only one they should be looking for.

Because it's all true. I killed a lot of people that day.

I feel sick to my stomach, and it's not from the food. Well, not just the food.

"They're only offering fifty million for me," PC pouts.

"Only sixty for me," Taka offers helpfully, but that only gets a glare from PC who angrily gestures to the hologram.

"Daisy's at a hundred, Orion's at two. Hell, even Oliver is at a fifty-five million." The cabin boy in question gulps loudly.

"It is not a competition," Orion mutters.

"Says the android who's beating me," PC exclaims.

I sigh and rub my temples. "Are we really talking about this right now?"

But a smile pulls at PC's lips, and I realize that he's trying to take my mind off everything. We all have to know the horrible truth about our faces being plastered all over the galaxy, but he's at least trying to take the sting out of it.

"No one's getting turned in," I say shortly. Unless it's me, but I don't say that out loud or otherwise hint at that possibility. "So long as we stay mobile, we stay vigilant, we can keep out of the Feds' and corporations' clutches."

"They will forget us as soon as there is another big crisis," Orion says, although he doesn't sound sure of himself.

Daisy gives him a pointed look. "When have you known the corporations to give up anything?"

The answer is never, and silence falls on the table as we all think about whatever future we could possibly have for ourselves while being on the run. While we've been all right so far, we've been on edge for the past two months. Set adrift. On our own.

Away from civilization or anyone who would be tempted to turn us in.

"I guess this is a bad time to say that we are running low on radioactive cores," Orion says softly.

My entire body stills as I stare aghast at him. The rest of the table does the same.

"We *what?*" Daisy thunders.

"Fuel." Orion, for all his programming of human behavior, misses the hysteria in her voice and gives a nonchalant shrug. "We only have about a week's worth left before we run out."

"And when were you going to tell us that, Orion?" she hisses through clenched teeth.

Instantly, my retina tells me that my blood pressure has risen to unsafe levels. And a warning goes off, one that I'm dreading.

Shit, it's happening earlier and earlier.

I shoot to my feet, my biological knee weak from my shattered nerves. "I need to go," I say, my voice sounding more strained than I'd like. Everyone looks at me curiously.

"You okay, Clem?" PC asks.

"Yeah. I think dinner's making me sick."

It's a complete lie, but it's believable. I'm a ticking time bomb right now, and my crew has no idea. I'd like to keep it that way for as long as possible.

I point to Orion. "We'll continue this discussion in a bit, all right? Just as soon as I take care of this."

Not that I can take care of this by myself. I force a smile, trying to act normal, even though I'm feeling anything but.

I back away from the table and to the door.

"Clem?" PC asks again, his voice wavering.

"I'll be back," I say, before I turn. Once I'm in the hallway, I sprint to my quarters, which are on the opposite end of the *Pícara II*. My retina counts down until my barely contained quarantine of the Infinity Virus raging through my body fails and I infect everyone and everything on this ship.

Yeah, that would be very bad.

I punch the lock on my door with my mechanical hand, and it irises open in response. I make sure to double-lock it behind me so that no one can get in or follow me. I don't want them to see what happens next.

I feel along the smooth walls of my room, feeling for a loose panel. My fingers find the seam, and I pry it away, revealing a secret compartment where I've been keeping the backpack I stole from Syn-Tech. It contains every vial of vaccine that I could get my hands on.

I pull it out and unzip the pack, revealing what remains of my stash of inoculations. The answer—not enough. Nowhere near enough to keep the virus at bay for long. After two months of keeping the virus on a tight leash, I guess I have about a month left before I run out.

And beyond that...well, I need to figure something out, although it's hard being on the run. I take out a syringe, measure out the correct amount of fluid, stick it into the fleshy part of my arm, and drive the plunger home.

I lean against the wall, panting. Hoping that it still works. There's a growing fear inside of me that one day, I'll inoculate myself and it won't work.

Please don't let it be today.

But there's no taunting voice in my head. Nothing infects the environment around me.

I close my eyes, resting my chin on my chest, trying to slow my heartbeat. My systems release a dose of serotonin to help calm me, meaning that I was close to panicking. I sigh and rub at my eyes. "Dammit," I mutter softly. "Dammit."

I don't know what I'll do in a month. I should be trying to find a cure. I should be out there, doing everything I can to save myself.

The truth is, I'm scared. I don't know what to do, or how I'll be able to fix this. I'm fairly certain that I killed everyone back on Alpha who had an inkling of what to do.

Is there any hope left for me?

I'm afraid of telling my crew. Because I know they'll want to do everything possible to save me. But I don't know if I can be saved. Or if I'm worth saving at this point.

Clementine Jones. 52.8% machine. 47.2% human. 100% cold-hearted killer.

And all coward.

I curl up my legs to my chest and rock myself gently. *It's going to be okay. It's going to be okay. It's going to be okay.*

But I know it won't be.

The lights in my quarters dim to almost a somber mood. I sigh and look up, knowing that the ship is responding to my distress. The *Pícara II* sees everything that happens on her, so I'm sure she knows exactly what I'm going through.

And she's trying to comfort me.

"Thank you," I whisper with a grim smile. "Thank you."

I sit there for a long, long time.

PREORDER NOW

Read more in The Infinity Project Universe

THE COURTESAN'S GALAXY

Read more in The Infinity Project Universe

Part robot, part slave, and all human, Felicity has been working as a courtesan to pay off her debt to the person who saved her life.

But when four men from her past come to her, she may find another way out.

GET IT NOW

SPACE SMUGGLERS ACADEMY: ELEMENTAL RUNNER

The galaxy's finest train at the prestigious school for Feds.
The rejects go to Space Smugglers Academy.
Guess which group I belong to.
I was once the most promising space cadet for the Feds, but

Read more in The Infinity Project Universe

then I was in a freak accident. Now instead of doing battle simulations, I can bend metal with my mind, and I can't control it.

So they kicked me out.

Then the very-illegal Space Smugglers Academy takes me in, hiding me in the darkest corner of the galaxy. I'm with students who are just as brilliant and messed up as me, including the Nova brothers who look to me as their captain and girlfriend.

The more I learn about my new powers and the true nature of the galaxy's government, the more I realize that they need to be stopped.

Because we're no longer rejects. We're rebels. And the revolution is about to start.

Space Smugglers Academy is the first book in a trilogy set in the same universe as *The Infinity Project*.

PREORDER IT NOW

About the Author

New York Times Bestselling Author Erin Hayes writes what she wants to read, which includes paranormal romance, contemporary romance, and urban fantasy sprinkled with vampires, billionaire princes, mermaids, steampunk and all the stuff you love.

She lives in San Francisco with her husband and a giant cat, along with too many Sailor Moon figurines and pieces of art she brought back from her travels. When she's not writing, well, she's planning her next big trip or watching sci-fi movies.

And if you like Star Wars, we're already best friends.

Follow her on:
www.erinhayesbooks.com
www.facebook.com/erinhayesbooks
Join my street team at: http://www.facebook.com/groups/erinsnerdcrew/

Made in the USA
Columbia, SC
27 August 2020